BUSCADERO

G·K
Hall
&Cº

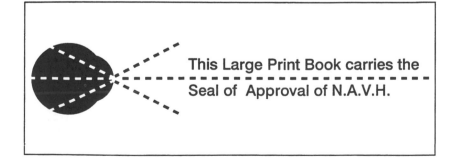

This Large Print Book carries the
Seal of Approval of N.A.V.H.

BUSCADERO

Bill Brooks

G.K. Hall & Co.
Thorndike, Maine

Published in Larbe Print by arrangement with
M. Evans & Company, Inc.

G.K. Hall Large Print Book Series.

Set in 16 pt. News Plantin by Minnie B. Raven.

Printed in the United States on acid-free,
high-opacity paper. ∞

Library of Congress Cataloging in Publication Data

Brooks, Bill, 1943–
    Buscadero / Bill Brooks
       p.   cm.
    ISBN 0-8161-5858-4 (alk. paper : lg. print)
    1. Large type books. I. Title.
    [PS3552.R65863B87 1993b]
    813'.54—dc20   93-20784

Dedicated to the Memory
of my parents,
Mary and Albert

Chapter One

He found McKinnon along the road just outside of Big River. It wasn't hard to spot a dead man out in the middle of nowhere. The ravages of time, critters, and heat, made it difficult to recognize an old friend. It had come down to the missing tip of the little finger on the right hand — McKinnon had lost it during a shootout at Dry Wells. Henry Dollar knew, he had been there too.

Having no shovel, the Texas Ranger was forced to gather rocks and build what grave he could — it was a grim task that took the better part of an hour.

The sun was the way the sun usually was in west Texas — hot. By the time he had finished, sweat was soaking through his shirt and his throat was parched. He pulled the canteen from his saddle horn and squatted on his heels near the crude grave.

The water tasted warm and mossy but it cut through the dust in his mouth and he was glad for it. He listened to the silence for a spell as he sat there staring at the mound of rocks that was all the legacy left for his friend and fellow ranger. It wasn't much, but Henry Dollar knew of many a man who had died in the service of the great state of Texas with little more than a mound of earth from which a handmade cross poked upward. And even that small tribute was blown away with the first hard Texas wind.

He didn't know any true Bible words to speak, never spent much time in church. He didn't even know any poems that would fit the solemnity of the moment. But reason and compassion dictated that he at least try. A man shouldn't just pass from this life to the next without something good said about him.

He swallowed another mouthful of water, lifted the battered gray Stetson from atop his head and stood up.

"I'll miss you, Jim, that's a fact. We'll all miss you. I know you had a sister up in Wichita, I'll make sure she's told." He paused, searching for the right words, remembering the times he'd shared with Jim McKinnon.

"You wasn't much of a cook when we broke trail together. Same could be said for your singing — it's a good thing we never herded cattle. Your night singing would've scared them halfway to Mexico." It seemed easier to remember the good times than the bad.

"But, you was always the first one through the door and the last one to come in out of the rain whenever we was chasing desperados. And if you hadn't been such a good shot, I'd probably been dead a long time ago. This damned old dusty place is going to be a lot more empty without you in it."

He let the words be carried off by the wind; for this one solitary moment, it seemed to blow in a gentle whisper.

He slapped what dust he could out of his Stetson and settled it back on his head knowing that he had said the best he could — what one fellow could say about another and not be lying. He hoped the good Lord would forgive him for being so ignorant on such an occasion.

He mounted the buckskin and reined its head north, toward the town of Big River. He had only passed through once — five years ago bringing a prisoner back from Mexico. He remembered it as a disappointment. He knew it to be not far, and it was only reasonable to believe that someone living up there might know something about a murdered Texas Ranger practically on their doorstep.

The town stood as a collection of shanties, of old weathered wood blistered gray and curling away from the rusted nails that tried to hold them together. He could throw a fair size rock from one end to the other. Mangy hounds came from out of whatever spots of shade they had been lying in and fell in behind the buckskin in a barking parade for a few yards, and then drifted back off to their shade to await another arrival.

He felt the stares from the open windows, and noticed as well the shaded gazes of men lounging up against those weary old buildings. He wasn't concerned as long as there was no sudden movement among them.

The gents of Big River — those cooling their heels that day along the broad and only street — saw the stranger riding up on the big buckskin

9

gelding. They saw too, the hand-tooled, double-rigged saddle that had the initials HD stamped on the skirt.

The saddle may have been fancy, but the man who sat it was not. He was a big man who rode ramrod straight, no slump to his back. His growth of beard glinted red in the sun, and showed flecks of gray.

It was hard for the onlookers to tell about the man's eyes, shaded as they were under a high-crowned Stetson that looked as though maybe every horse in Texas had stomped on it at one time or another. But, the eyes seemed to be staring at something that wasn't there — the way a rattler's eyes are just before he strikes.

The stranger wore a long linen duster that had collected the dust of the Panhandle. His boots were scarred but not run-down at the heels. He wore big Mexican spurs whose rowels were the size of silver dollars.

No one that was watching the stranger could tell, because of the long linen duster he wore, that beneath it he wore a Remington .44-40 revolver with a six-inch barrel strapped to his hip. It had a beaded sight and had stag horn grips. He also wore a hide-out pistol, a Colt's Lightening .41 caliber pistol.

The hardwood stock of a Winchester repeating rifle protruded from his saddle boot.

The stranger's arrival seemed to have triggered a silence, a stillness about the town. Only the clop of the buckskin's hooves on the hardpan street, and the clatter of blades from the town's windmill buffeting in the wind could be heard.

He reined up to a whiskey tent. Whiskey peddlers knew most everything that there was worth knowing about a town and its folks. Whiskey peddlers and barbers. He hadn't seen any barber shops on the way in, although he had spotted one fellow wearing knee-high boots, sitting in a busted chair, and holding a bowl atop his head while another fellow cut his hair with a pair of scissors.

"Don't wander off, Ike," he said to the buckskin as he dismounted and dropped the reins to the ground. The horse eyed him and lifted its head, shaking dust out of its mane.

As shebangs go, the whiskey tent seemed to fit the bill: a simple affair with a few chairs and a plank of raw lumber laid across the tops of two big whiskey barrels to serve as a bar. No beer, no bitters, just whiskey, and just one kind at that. In this case, it was a brand called Black Stump. At least that's what the labels on the bottles read.

The bartender had the consumptive look of a lot of men who had drifted west. He wore a bowler and had a pocked face and bad teeth. One eye was bad, milked over and unseeing.

"Whiskey's four bits, mister," said the bardog. "A whole bottle'll cost you ten dollars."

"I take it this is the only place in town to get a drink?" said Henry Dollar, knowing that the price was a gouging.

"Hell there, bucko, this is the only place in a hundirt miles to git a drink!" When the bardog opened his mouth to laugh, the ranger saw just how bad his teeth were.

Without pulling the duster back far enough to expose the badge or the Remington, Henry Dollar retrieved four bits from his pocket and placed them on the bar.

He sipped his whiskey in silence and noticed that his presence was being observed by the handful of drinkers within the tent. He didn't recognize any of the grim silent faces. But then, Texas was a big country and he hadn't expected to.

Maybe McKinnon's killer was one of these men, maybe not. The hot wind beat against the sides of the tent with the rhythm of someone spanking dust out of a rug.

The bardog watched him sip his whiskey with idle curiosity and picked at something at the base of his neck. Henry didn't care for the man's manner or presence, to say nothing of the way he smelled in such close quarters. He finished the whiskey and shoved the empty glass across the plank.

"Where's your law around here?"

"Is that some sort of a trick question, mister?" The barkeeper seemed amused.

"Wasn't meant to be."

"Wah, mister, we ain't got no law in Big River, just like we ain't got no river in Big River. The law and the river done both dried up and blowed away. We had us a constable one time — old Jake Evers. Thought he'd up and be a big crow hearabouts. Rid all the way down to Amirilly and bought him a badge and a six shooter and appointed hisself Constable.

"Har! That was a hoot. First drunken cowboy to hit town shot ol' Jake through the lungs. Last law we ever had. At least it has been so far."

"Well, it must keep things interesting for everybody," said Henry. He shifted his weight and turned to leave.

Three men appeared in the opening of the whiskey tent. The pewter light outside cast them in silhouette, obscuring their faces. He waited for them to pass before leaving. They held their ground. He gave it a second more. Finally, they came inside, the rhythm of their movement announced by their spurs. Each man carried a sidearm high on the hip. He started past them toward the tent's opening.

"You from around here?" asked one of the trio. Henry turned slowly. They stood there, slack-shouldered and unkempt. He knew their sort. Tramps. Take-down artists looking to prey on the weak or ill-prepared.

"I axed, are you from around here?" The man doing the talking appeared the oldest of the three, heavy around the middle, moon-faced — he wore a sombrero. The two flanking him stood with their thumbs hooked inside their cartridge belts. Their half sneers reminded the ranger of the mangy hounds that had come out to greet him on the street — a lot of bark but no bite.

"Just passing through." He would not ordinarily have tolerated such inquisition from men such as

13

these, but he had come here looking for something, and maybe he was looking at the something he had come here for.

"Where'd you be passing to?" asked the fat man.

Henry shifted his stance for better balance. Balance in a gunfight was a lot of what kept you alive.

"Ain't sure. I'm just looking for a friend of mine. He's a young fellow — good-looking boy. Goes by the name of J.T. McKinnon. Any of you seen a man like that?"

He saw Fatty's jaw muscles knot up.

"Naw, we ain't seed nobody like that," said the tall ugly man to Fatty's right. Henry noticed that the third man, the one standing to the left of Fatty, had shifted his hand closer to his pistol.

"You're pretty sure you haven't seen this fellow?"

"We already said we ain't," said Fatty. "You sound like maybe you're the law or somptin?"

"No, I'm just passing through, like I said. Looking for this ol' friend of mine. Rides a long-legged sorrel, real nice gaited animal."

The eyes of the fat man shifted to those of the tall ugly one before returning Henry's gaze. "No sir, we ain't seen nobody like you describe. We'd a remembered a feller like that. Just like we spotted that big buckskin outside with that fancy saddle on it. That your rig, mister?"

Henry looked past the trio toward the bartender. "You got a hotel or a rooming house here in Big River?"

14

"There's the Little Star just up the street — it ain't but a place to flop and a plate of beans, but some call it a hotel." He gave a toothy grin.

Henry nodded his appreciation and gave the fat man and his two friends a final hard look before making his departure. Once outside, the heat and light caused him to squint — seemed like if you lived in Texas, you spent a lot of time squinting.

He walked Ike down the street until he came to the Little Star. The bardog had been right; it wouldn't hardly pass for a hotel in anyplace except the Texas Panhandle.

Henry grasped the porcelain door knob and turned it; the whole door seemed to rattle in his hand as he opened it and stepped inside.

A hunched-backed man was sitting on a three-legged stool near a smudgy window and holding a newspaper up to it in order to see the print. He looked up and stared at the intruder through thick, wire-rimmed spectacles.

"Sompin I can help you with?"

"I'll need a room for the night."

The clerk's mouth turned rubbery in its effort to smile. "Well now, you come to the right place, mister."

"I hear it's the only place."

"That's a born fact. You want a mattress with your room? A mattress will be two bits extry. You want to just toss down your warbag, sleep on the floor, it'll cost you less. Martress's is clean, though. I air 'em out ever week or so — no graybacks crawlin' around in 'em, and they's made of good

15

shuck so's to give a man comfort."

"I'll take a room and a mattress," said Henry.

"Yes sir!" said the hunchback, putting down the paper and moving over to a small desk. "That'll be one dollar and twenty-five cents for room and mattress for the night."

Henry dug the money out of his pocket, this time being less careful about pulling his duster back. The clerk noticed the big Remington and the bulge of another pistol.

"You're well heeled," he said.

"It's a hard country."

The hunchback grinned. "It is indeed."

"I'll need care for my horse, is there a livery hereabouts?"

"Just up the street. Jesus Ortega knows horses like most men know their wives."

"I'll be back. Make sure all the ticks and bedbugs are shook out of that mattress. I don't like sharing quarters." The hunchback's eyes rolled behind the thick glasses.

Henry found the livery. An old Mexican dozed on a cane-bottom chair that had most of the cane frayed out.

"Hola," said Henry, loud enough to stir the man from whatever place he had drifted off to.

The old man's lids fluttered open and he rubbed one eye. He looked older than the land itself. The old man's eyes went right to Henry's buckskin.

"Hees a fine animal, señor."

"Sí. I want him watered, fed, and brushed down."

16

"Right thees way, señor." He lifted himself from the stool and led the way inside the stables. The old Mexican walked like a man who hadn't spent much time off of the back of a horse. His short, wiry frame included legs so bowled sheep could run through them.

The interior of the stable was cool, the smell of horse and hay pleasant. The old man led them to an empty stall. Henry removed Ike's saddle and bridle and then spanked him inside.

"I'll be here first thing in the morning," Henry said as he slipped the old man a silver dollar. The old man looked at it laying in his brown palm.

"I'll take good care of him, señor." Henry turned to leave when one of the horses caught his eye: A tall, long-legged sorrel. He walked over and inspected the right flank of the animal. A welt of initials branded into the sorrel's hide confirmed his suspicions: JM.

"Who brought this animal in here?" he asked the old man.

"That is meester Ned Butcher's horse, señor."

"Where would I find this fellow, Ned Butcher?"

"Oh, he's easy to find, señor. He's big and round and he has oogly friends." The old man spat brown juice and grinned.

"He jus' went over to get himself a drink. He and hees oogly friends they like to drink and have a good time."

"This fellow wear a big sombrero?"

"Sí, tha's heem."

The old Mexican wrangler saw the tall gringo

17

shift the right side of his duster back, exposing the pistol on his hip as he crossed the street toward the whiskey tent. He heard the clear ringing of the big spurs with each step the stranger took.

Henry Dollar checked the load in both pistols as he crossed the street toward the whiskey tent. Satisfied, he replaced them in their holsters.

Ned Butcher and his two companions were hossing one another when Henry re-entered.

"I just found my friend's sorrel over in the stables. The Mexican said it was yours!"

The three of them turned, their hands reaching for their pistols. Henry shot the fat man through the chest, the slug spanking up dust and slamming him against the plank bar, his weight snapping the board and spilling glasses.

The quiet one had cleared his piece and snapped the trigger, but the move had been too quick and his shot went wide of its mark punching a hole through the side of the tent instead of the ranger.

In a swift but deliberate move that took less time than a breath, Henry Dollar brought the Remington to bear on the tall man whose own finger was pressing the trigger of his pistol for the second shot. The ranger's slug tore through jawbone on its way toward its final destruction. The tall man's body fell atop that of his fat friend.

The ugly one had dropped his own pistol in fear and was scrambling for the scattergun that the bardog kept propped up against the back wall of the tent. He swung it up, the twin black eyes coming to bear on the ranger, but it was way too late.

18

The ranger's shot took him dead center, spinning him around. He crashed into the side of the tent, his hands clawing at the canvas as he slid to his knees and then toppled over face down.

A smoking pistol in each hand, the ranger brought his gaze to rest on the only man left in the whiskey tent — the pock-faced bardog. The man shoved both hands into the air.

"I just serve them liquor," he stammered. "I ain't married to them!"

The tent was filled with the acrid smoke of gun-fire. The wind pounded against the canvas walls as though trying to get in. Henry knelt next to each of the dead men and searched their pockets.

He found Jim McKinnon's Texas Ranger badge in the vest pocket of the fat man. It had a smear of dried blood on it. Henry wiped it clean and put it inside his own pocket.

He stood and eyed the sweating bartender.

"You take whatever money you find on them and use it to get them buried," ordered Henry. "Send your burying man out west of town to where a pile of rocks stand and have him dig a proper grave for that fellow there. Make sure he puts up a marker."

"What you want it to say?"

"J.T. McKinnon. Texas Ranger."

"That all?"

"That's enough."

Chapter Two

Johnny Montana dreamt of rivers — rivers that raged and roared and overflowed their banks. He dreamt of being astride a horse, trying to cross such a river. In the dream, the water tugs at his legs and keeps rising, churning, and swirling until it reaches his waist. The water is cold, like ice, and hurts like needles piercing his skin.

He is in the middle of the river — the shore far away. He can feel the horse floundering beneath him, feel the panic set into the animal's flesh and then his own. And then, the water is separating him from the horse, unseating him and he desperately tries to hold on.

The horse rolls over in the current, surfaces again, its eyes white with terror, and then is swept away downstream.

The turgid brown waters pull at him, his feet dancing below him trying to touch bottom, but there is no bottom. He regrets that he never learned to swim, feels a great sadness along with the terrible, terrible fear, and the waters suck him under, choking away his breath, choking away his hope.

He struggled awake, sat bolt upright in a start. The light inside the jacal was dim. Through an open window on the east wall, he could see a thin blade of pearl light knifing across the horizon and realized that it was near dawn.

20

His heart pounded wildly inside his chest; the dream had not left his mind.

A woman stirred on the bed beside him; the corn husk mattress cracked with every movement. He reached for her. She came awake to his touch.

"What . . . ?"

He shook his head and reached for the bottle of tequila on the chair next to the bed, uncorked it, put it to his lips, and swallowed long and hard.

"It's the dreams," he told her. The tequila burned his lips. "I was dreaming about a river. I was drowning in it, same as always."

"It's just a dream, Johnny," she told him.

"Dreams have a way of coming true," he said, his gaze focused on the dawn coming through the small square window.

"My daddy told me dreams never do come true," said the woman. She was pretty, her hair long and auburn, but dark in dim light. She had milk white skin, small breasts, and slender legs. The sound of her voice carried with it the mellow sweetness of the South. She raised her hand and stroked his hair, which was damp with sweat.

"Your daddy don't know anything!" he told her, his voice edgy and tense. "Dreams have a way of coming true, at least in my family they do."

He swallowed more of the tequila and sat up on the side of the bed, letting his feet dangle just above the earthen floor. In spite of the hour, the air was warm and still.

He continued the litany on dreams: "All men who live by their wits and their guns have it in

21

them to read dreams. Jesse James had it. John Wesley Hardin had it, too. My family's got it, and I got it. Only a fool would ignore his dreams!"

She could smell his fear and it made her fearful, too.

"I tell you, Kate, I'm going to drown in a river someday, and there ain't nothing going to save me when that day comes."

She did what she could to calm him.

"You won't die, Johnny, if we don't cross anymore rivers," she told him.

"Don't cross anymore rivers!" His anger came out in hot, sour gasps. "Hell, woman, how are we going to travel if we don't cross anymore rivers! This whole dern country is full of rivers!"

She was fully awake now. He could be mean to live with when he was upset. She touched the bare skin on his back with her finger tips.

"We could just go around any rivers we come across," she said, believing in the logic of it.

He swallowed more tequila and leaned back against the cool adobe wall of the jacal.

"Katie, I know you mean well, but there are some things you don't know a thing about."

"Like what?"

"Like crossing rivers. You just can't go around every river you come up on — some of them dang things is hundreds of miles long."

She knew he wouldn't let the subject rest until a solution could be found.

"Well, maybe we ought to just find a place and settle down, someplace where we don't ever have to worry about crossing rivers."

"Well, maybe we ought to!" he told her, drinking the last of the tequila, feeling its fire in his throat.

"But, right now we can't do that — we're wanted all over the territory. Outlaws don't just quit running and settle down when they want to and not ever cross rivers again. Heck, we tried something like that, the law would be on us like ticks on a festered hound."

"What are we going to do then, Johnny?" she asked, feeling uncomfortable with what he was telling her. She was struck with how much things had changed in the last three months, from the time she first met him until now.

"If you are afraid to cross rivers, and we can't settle down, what are we going to do?"

"I didn't say I was afraid to cross rivers," he said bitterly. "I said, I hated crossing them. That's a big difference."

Johnny Montana was the handsomest man that Katie Swensen had ever met. He was tall and dark and sported a thin, neatly trimmed moustache, and he had midnight black eyes. He was particular about his person; he shaved regularly, put rosewater in his hair, and preferred clean shirts when he could get them, which wasn't often because they were on the trail so much of the time.

It had all happened so suddenly, their meeting. She considered it destiny.

He had come into her daddy's dry goods store

where she clerked — Tallapoosa County, Alabama — to try on hats. He was leaning toward a short-brimmed Stetson when he first caught her eye, and she his.

"How do I look?" he asked. He had a smile that would melt ice.

Later that same day, they found themselves eating ice cream in a small confectionery store named WENZE'S, and that was when he had told her how pretty she was.

"Ain't never seen anything like you," he said. "A woman like you could steal a man's heart without even trying."

They talked until it had grown dark and then he walked her home. When he came again the next day to the store she wasn't at all that surprised. She was already in love with him.

"I guess I can be a pest," he had said. And then he asked her a question that changed everything about her life.

"You planning on sticking around these parts the rest of your life?" She knew instantly that if he asked her to go, she would: Men like Johnny Montana did not come through Tallapoosa County every day.

They left in the late hours of a warm evening, her daddy snoring in the other room. It all seemed like such a grand adventure.

It wasn't until days later, after a few stickups along the way, that he told her about having killed a man back in Alabama. The news cut her like a knife.

24

"He was just some ol' pig farmer I got into a row with," was the way Johnny Montana put it to her. "He may have been good at raising hogs, but he wasn't worth a tinker's damn at gambling." She wanted hard to believe him and to take his side in it, but still it blunted something about the way she felt about him.

"Anyway, it don't matter — it was a fair fight, everyone saw it, said so. I just wanted you to know that's all."

She wondered at the time why he told her. She came to understand more fully after she witnessed him pulling a robbery along the road of a man travelling alone and on horseback.

She wept and he tried comforting her. He told her it was all necessary and the worst was simply that he had relieved somebody of a few dollars and that no one would be the worse for it.

"Johnny, I don't know if I can live this way," she said after the first time she waited in the bushes while he stepped out in front of the horseman and robbed him.

"It's only a temporary thing," he told her. "Only until we get to Texas. There's lots of opportunity in Texas and I won't have to do this sort of thing anymore."

She wanted to believe him. He had won her heart so completely, and she wasn't the kind of person just to give up on the man she loved, so she stayed with him and sometimes cried because of her loneliness for her papa back in Tallapoosa County.

They crossed country and made it to Ft. Smith,

25

Arkansas. She didn't care much for the place, it was full of rough men, smelly air, and wildness. She urged that they keep moving.

"You said you wanted to go to Texas," she told him, but it was just the sort of place he took to. He rented a room and put her in it.

"I think I can double our money, and if so, we'll go to Texas in style," he said. She knew what he meant. Aside from road agentry, Johnny was a gambler. He lost everything that first night and they had to sneak out of the hotel in the dark because he had no money to pay the bill.

It was later that same day, several miles outside of Ft. Smith, that Johnny paused and said he thought he heard someone coming down the road. He took out his silk handkerchief and laid it on the ground and put his ear against it.

"Somebody's coming for sure," he said. "Climb off into those weeds yonder and wait."

A man came riding a beautiful Arabian horse with a dish face. The man was well-dressed and wore a broad beaver hat. Johnny stood there holding his arm as though he had been hurt. She watched the whole thing from the tall grass she had gone to stand in.

When the man reined his horse up to where Johnny was standing, she heard the man say, "Are you alright, mister?" And then Johnny pulled out his pistol and told the man to throw up his hands because he was being robbed.

Instead of putting his hands into the air, the man started to reach for something inside his coat, and Johnny shot him. She saw the man slump from the saddle and drop to the ground, heard him groan once and try to get up.

"Damn fool!" Johnny shouted as he grabbed the reins of the Arabian in one hand before it could run off. He had aimed his pistol at the man's head by the time she came running out of the weeds.

"Don't you shoot that man again, damn you!" she shouted at him. Her horror over what she had witnessed left her angry beyond belief.

She saw how he looked up at her, his face a mask of confusion, of uncertainty at the hellcat that was running out of the bushes toward him, screaming and waving her arms.

"You shoot him again," she shouted, "I'll leave you and go back to Ft. Smith and tell them what you have done!"

He didn't quarrel with her. Instead, he lowered his pistol and told her he was sorry any of this had happened. She wasn't sure whether to believe him or not.

"If you was watching," he said, "you know I didn't shoot him on purpose. He was reaching for his gun to shoot me!" He said it like a little boy scolded and trying to defend himself. She looked from the dark smoldering eyes of Johnny to the ashen face of the man lying on the ground.

"We have to do something," she said.

"Ain't nothing we can do except get out of here fast," he ordered.

"We can't just leave him, he'll die out here — look how he's bleeding."

"Someone will come along and help him. It can't be us. They'd put us both in jail, sweetie. That's something you don't want to have to experience." The whole time, he searched the man's pockets, producing a wallet and a small nickel-plated pistol.

"See, I told you he was going for his gun!"

The revolver was a .36 caliber Navy Colt pocket gun with fancy scroll work and the words *Presented To The Hon. W.F. Gray* engraved on the butt strap.

There had been nearly one hundred dollars in the wallet.

"I guess we lucked out," said Johnny. "This fellow must've been important."

Later, Johnny sold the horse for five hundred dollars, and after that, they took a river boat up the Sabine River. Johnny gambled and spent freely, so that by the time they landed in Magnolia Springs, they were nearly broke again.

He spent what little they had left on a pair of poor saddle horses. Texas was what Johnny had wanted, and she hoped that now that they had arrived, things would be different. He had talked it up so much.

But as they travelled west, it seemed as though Texas was a lot more of the same, only hotter and more desolate.

One night they stole crabapples from back of somebody's homestead and got cramps from eating them. A day later, Johnny robbed a man walking his mule along the dusty road they were on. The only valuable the man possessed was a nickel-plated Elgin pocket watch and two dimes.

Three days later, in Boleweevel, Texas, Johnny walked into a Chinese Laundry and stuck the fancy pistol in the sallow lace of the Celestial that worked there. Again, the pickings were poor: a jarful of Indian head pennies and some boiled shirts.

She thought Texas was the worst place she had ever been.

As the days wore on, and the nights turned black and cold as they lay on bedrolls on the ground, she began to feel sorry she had ever taken up with Johnny Montana. But it all seemed too late to change, and in spite of her remorse, there was still something about him that drew her to him.

But most of the time, it was hard for her to just keep drifting, and one evening as they sat around a fire of cow pies he had gathered, she felt forced to say something to him.

"I'd like it if you were to find a regular job, Johnny. You know, so we could settle down. I'm plain weary of always wandering. Even if you was to get some sort of cowboy work, I wouldn't mind so much."

"Cowboys!" he yelped. He had been trying to pull off his boots when she said it. Now, he ceased that effort and stared at her across the flickering firelight.

"Honey, I ain't no cowboy! Working for wages, looking at the back end of a cow — that ain't what Johnny Montana was born to do. If I had a been a cowboy to start with, you wouldn't have given me a second look the first time we laid eyes

29

on one another. So don't talk to me about cow-boys!"

Three days later, Johnny Montana robbed a small bank in Rawly of three hundred dollars. She would have to leave him soon.

She got up from the bed and walked to the window. The light was a soft gray, the air silent and still. She thought of her papa and wondered what he must be doing. What would he think of her, if he knew where she was at and what had happened in the space of the past few months? It made her sad to think of him.

"Come on back to bed, sweetie. Let ol' Johnny bring you some comfort, bring us both some comfort." Now that the tequila had washed away the last remnants of the dream, he was feeling better.

"I'm thinking that New Mexico territory is the place to go," he said. "Santa Fe, maybe. Lots of charm in Santa Fe. Pretty country I hear. Maybe I was wrong about Texas. It don't seem like we've had much luck at all."

She only half listened as he talked in that loose rambling way of his. She had grown weary of that, too. The dreams, the idle talk of better things ahead. She told herself that she could have even accepted the fact he was loose-footed and a dreamer. But, she could not be with a man who shot and robbed people and probably always would find it easier to take from others than to earn his own way.

In that sudden instant, she decided to tell him to go on without her. She turned away from the window just as a chunk of adobe casing blew up. Instinctively, she fell to the floor. A second shot whizzed through the open window and slammed into the wall just above the bed knocking pieces of mud plaster down into Johnny Montana's dark hair.

"Come on out with your hands empty!" shouted a voice from outside. "We are Texas Rangers, and you are completely surrounded! You've got about a minute before we cut loose!"

Johnny Montana had taken refuge under the bed, his pistol in his hand.

"What are we going to do, Johnny?" she cried.

He looked at her with his dark dark eyes and said, "I guess we finally been caught."

They were tough leathery men who escorted them into the ranger station at Pecos.

They were marched in and stood before a white-haired man sitting behind a desk. He had a snowy moustache that flowed downward past the corners of his mouth. His faded blue eyes lifted to gaze upon the couple standing before him. He had an instant of regret at seeing such a young woman wearing iron handcuffs.

One of the flanking rangers announced them.

"Trailed them from Rawly up to a line shack near Bad Water flats, Cap'n. Feller here says his name is Johnny Montana. Claims he's from Kansas. Claims he's innocent, too."

31

The ranger laid the nickel-plated Navy on the lawman's desk.

"He was carrying this, Cap'n. Got the name W.F. Gray on it."

The lawman's gaze came to rest on that of the woman. He held a wanted poster in his hand.

"I guess that seals it," he said. She was surprised at the softness of his voice.

"This is a wanted poster from Arkansas for the killing of a state senator." He glanced once at the engraving on the pistol. The senator's name was Willard Gray. "I hope you got more than this fancy pistol from him. It seems little to hang for."

She felt the sudden closeness of the room, the hard stares of the men around her. *It had all come to this.*

"You are also being arrested for the bank robbery at Rawly. And, I have received reports over the last few weeks that a couple fitting your description has robbed one Joe Turner in Wise County of his watch and twenty cents. And, a Chinaman was robbed in his laundry of a jar of pennies and some shirts."

Motes of dust danced in the light entering the room through open windows.

The lawman's gaze was unyielding.

"It pains me to see a woman in irons," he said simply.

She felt herself falling, felt the strong steady hands holding her. She was carried to a cot in one of the cells.

Ben Goodlow turned his attention to the man.

"What sort of a man would drag a young girl like that along with him while he robs and kills people, is what I'd like to know?"

Johnny stared into the unflinching eyes of the lawman and knew instantly not to irritate this man.

"You are a bad piece of work, mister — I've hunted down trash like you my whole life." The ranger's words were strung taut as strained ropes.

"Soon as I can get you in front of the circuit judge, I'm requesting you get sent back to Arkansas for the killing of that state senator. I got a feeling that Judge Parker, back there in Ft. Smith, will make sure your wild days come to an end."

"You can't do that!" shouted Johnny Montana. "This is Texas, this ain't Arkansas. The jurisdiction's different."

"Sounds like you studied the law some?"

"I have."

"Then you didn't study enough. Here in Texas, I represent the law, and so do my men. I say you go back, you go back."

"That's something the judge'll have to decide."

"Don't get sassy, son. The judge is a brother-in-law of mine. I reckon he'll take under advisement any suggestions I have to make."

"This is a damn sorry thing," said the outlaw.

"No, boy, this is Texas."

Chapter Three

Autauga County, Alabama

Wes Biggs had been the most successful hog farmer in Autauga County clear up until the day Johnny Montana shot him once in the forehead during an argument over a card game.

He died wearing bib coveralls, a green shirt, and a scuffed pair of brogans that had dried pig muck on them.

In spite of the success he had known as a hog farmer, Wes Biggs' funeral was a simple affair. The only extravagance was a custom-built coffin cut of cedar; Wes Biggs was a big man and there wasn't a ready-made coffin in all of Autauga County big enough to hold him. The coffin had cost seventy dollars and sported brass handles.

The dead man's two grown sons, Lowell and Carter, wept like babies when the heavy coffin was lowered into the grave of sandy loam.

A great crowd had gathered for the funeral at the Biggs farm. And once, during the graveside prayer, the wind shifted in a fashion that brought it from the direction of the pig lots. The smell got embarrassing, but no one put up a fuss on such a solemn occasion, even though the odor caused eyes to smart. Some of the women lifted tiny white hankies to their noses, pretending to dab at their eyes.

Three of Wes Biggs's prize blue shoat hogs were

butchered and roasted over pits of hot coals in order to feed the crowd.

Cooking the hogs had begun the night before, and by the time the burying was over, the meat had burned black on the outside but came off in pink moist slabs when cut and laid on plates.

Lowell and Carter thought that everyone was enjoying themselves at their daddy's expense, but Southern upbringing had taught them to refrain from showing their displeasure.

"I guess we got enough hogs that eating three won't make that much a difference," said Lowell over a mouthful of the sweet tasting pork.

"I guess not," said Carter. "I just wish Daddy was here to enjoy it with us."

It seemed like a long time before everyone finally drifted off. All the men came up and shook Lowell and Carter's hands, and most of the women kissed the boys on their cheeks before heading off to their buggies and horses.

When the last of the crowd had left, Lowell and Carter sat on the steps of their daddy's house and watched it grow dark; they could hear frogs croaking down in a pond below the house — the croaks sounded like questions: *Now what! Now what!*

"We've got to make a choice, Lowell," said the older of the two brothers.

"What sort of choice?"

"It's been eatin' at me ever since that sumabitch, Johnny Montana murdered Pa!" Carter's face was full and pink like his daddy's had been, like the pinkness of cooked hog meat.

35

"We can stay here and raise pigs the rest of our lives, and make out like nothin's happened, act like the old man's blood being spilt don't mean a thing . . . or, we can go after that sumabitch and bury him in the ground!"

Lowell stared off into the dark purple haze of dusk, and saw a shadowy landscape that no longer felt familiar.

His words came out thick and slow, like the land itself, like the sluggish rivers, like a hound dog walking down a dirt road on a summer's day.

"I'm with ya, Carter, you know that. Family has to stick together. But, we ain't gunmen. Ain't neither one of us ever killed nothin' but a hog in all our lives. We catch hold of Johnny Montana, he's liable to be more than we can stand."

Lowell was a leaner, taller man than his brother. His face was ridged with bone. His knuckles and wrists and elbows were ridged with bone. He was bone and sinew and black restless eyes. His ridge of jawbone worked under the knotted muscle as he sat there contemplating the darkness, contemplating Carter's suggestion.

"Well, if you're with me then I say good. I can't see just doin' nothin'. Raising hogs don't mean a thing to me anymore!"

"Maybe we could hire us a man to go after Montana," said Lowell.

"Hire somebody! Like who would *we* hire?"

"Maybe we could hire ol' Knife Davis," said Lowell, shifting his long bony legs and stretching his back. "Everyone knows that ol' Knife killed

36

some boys down around the Gulf. Killed them over liquor, or some such. A man like that don't mind killing so much. Probably could get ol' Knife to do the job for a hundred dollars, maybe less."

"Knife Davis is a drunkard and can't be trusted," said Carter. He could smell the pigs now that the wind had shifted, could hear their rooting and squealing. Pigs, he thought. God damn hogs! It felt like a fire in his belly.

Carter swung his bulk down off the porch and stood in the yard staring off at something Lowell knew wasn't there. Without turning to look at his brother, Carter said: "Besides, I won't pay any man to take care of our family business. Either we do this thing ourselves, or we just let it go!"

"What about the farm?" asked Lowell. "What about the hogs?"

"We'll get cousin Ed to tend to it."

"How we going to find Johnny Montana, Carter?"

"We'll find him. He bragged around about how he was goin' to go to Texas. Hell, Texas can't be all that big."

"He's got a week's start on us."

"Yeah, but he don't know we're even after him, probably never figure in his life that a couple of hog farmers would try and track him down."

"Probably not," said Lowell. "Least not us."

The body of State Senator Willard F. Gray lay in a black mahogany casket that had silver handles and silver palm leaves on the lid. His hair had been combed and parted with rosewater; his gaunt, stone face had traces of white powder in the hollows of his cheeks. He wore a boiled shirt with a paper collar and pearl buttons, a black suit with velvet lapels and black silk trim; his hands looked as though they had been sculpted out of wax.

There was no evidence whatsoever of the small black hole that Johnny Montana's bullet had made just below the senator's right nipple.

Constituents, friends, and strangers came to view the body as it rested on a catafalque directly beneath the dome of the state capitol building; their footsteps echoed on the marble floor as they passed by.

After three days of Lying-In-State at the capitol building in Little Rock, a train carried the senator's body to his home in Montgomery County for burial in the misty beauty of the Ozarks.

His widow and two grown daughters watched as the ornate casket was lowered into the ground. All three women wept beneath their black veils, and they were given the state flag that had draped his coffin by a uniformed member of the Little Rock Militia who had accompanied the senator's body home.

And then, just as the coffin was lowered into the dark shaft of grave, it began to rain a light cold rain that chilled the skin and splattered darkly against the clothes. All the food that had been placed on long wooden tables and covered with white linen had to be taken inside the big house.

"It's as though the Lord himself is shedding tears," said one woman whose black bonnet withstood the first drops of rain.

"He was a good man," replied a neighbor. "He did a lot for us back here in Montgomery County."

"Seems the country ain't safe for anyone anymore," said another man, who was working a chaw of tobacco inside his jaw and looking for a place to spit that wouldn't offend any of the mourners or the family.

"Seems like if they can shoot a man like Willard Gray, a state's senator, off'n his horse in broad daylight, they can damn near shoot anybody," continued the man, and then spat straight down between the toes of his boots.

"You ought not to chew at such an occasion," said the man's wife, looking consternated.

And then everybody went inside the big house to eat and to get out of the rain.

"Mrs. Gray," said a man in a checked suit. She knew the man to be George Kimbel, a local banker and trusted friend of her late husband's.

She stared at him through the veil. He could see her eyes were red from the crying.

"Mrs. Gray, if I might have a word with you in private?"

She led him into a small sideroom where the senator's favorite rocker sat empty; doilies rested on the rocker's arms.

"There are some of us who wish to assure that

justice is served in this terrible tragedy. Will was a trusted friend to all of us. Me and several others who wish to remain discreet have decided to post a reward for Will's murderer."

"That's very generous of you, Mr. Kimbel. But, as I understand it, the state of Arkansas has already posted a reward."

The banker coughed, cleared his throat politely and said, "Yes ma'am, we're well aware of that. Thing is, even if the guilty party is captured and returned, there is no way of assuring that justice will be served. Lots of guilty men have been set free, even under Judge Parker's court."

"I see, Mr. Kimbel. You think that maybe Will's killer might find a way to get off?"

"Anything's possible, Mrs. Gray. Our little, hmmm . . . , committee, would like to make sure that doesn't happen. I know a man that would probably be interested in the reward."

"You mean bounty?"

"Well, I reckon you could call it that. However, if you're opposed to the idea, we'll respect your wishes."

"No, Mr. Kimbel," she said, shaking her head slightly. "Maybe once all the sorrow has passed from me, I will find our conversation troubling. But right now, I'm about as full of anger and hate as I reckon I can be. And to tell you the truth, it would trouble me more to see Will's murderer go without punishment. You have my approval, sir."

"I'll see to it then."

"Hello in the cabin!"

Eli Stagg lifted his bearish head, the whiskers of his beard tangled about his face, his fierce wet eyes searching the sound outside.

"Who might it be?" he yelled out, reaching for the Hawkins rifle.

"Faustus, Eli. It's me, Faustus!"

The big man sat up on the side of his cot, reached for the Creedmore rifle leaning against the wall.

"What you want, coming around here?"

"Brought someone to see you, a gent. He's got some business he wants to discuss!"

The big man approached the door cautiously, cracked it open far enough to see. The morning light gathered in the reddish whiskers, giving them the color of dried blood.

"What sort of offer?"

"Well hell, if'n you'll let us come up to the cabin, I'll reckon you'll find out!"

Two men shared the wagon seat. The one doing the talking was Faustus Greenbush, a mountain man like himself. He and Faustus had shared camps and grub together, and now and then their liquor. But that was as far as it went. Eli Stagg maintained no friends.

The other man was well-dressed — a checked suit and a dandy little hat perched atop his head.

"This is Mr. Kimbel," announced Faustus with a mouth smeared and stained by tobaccojuice.

He saw the man Kimbel eye him, eye the rifle in his hands, whisper something to Faustus.

"Got no secrets around here," said Eli Stagg sternly, his fierce stare leaving no allowance for humor.

The man in the checked suit stiffened.

"I just told your friend here that you didn't seem prepared for company and that maybe we ought to return another time."

"Depends on your business."

"Like I told you, Eli. It's a money deal."

"Step on down then."

Eli Stagg produced a jug of sour mash from within the cabin and sat it on a stump. The three men stood around the stump and shared the liquor and talked about why Mr. Kimbel had come.

"Mr. Greenbush tells me you are very, very good at tracking and hunting," said George Kimbel.

"Let's cut to it, Mr. Kimbel. What is it you need doin' and how much you willin' to pay?"

Kimbel explained it.

"A thousand dollars just to find this feller and kill him?"

"That's correct. Of course, I'll want my name left out of the matter, and that of Mrs. Gray. As far as anyone else is concerned, we've never had this discussion."

"How much a reward is the state offerin'?"

"Five hundred, but only paid upon trial and conviction of the accused. Those whom I represent, Mr. Stagg, are not so much interested in trials as they are seeing that justice is served."

"I ain't a blind man, mister. I can see your point!"

"I am prepared to offer you one hundred dollars in advance, for travelling expenses if you will. The rest to be paid upon proof that the task has been carried out."

"Proof! What sort of proof!"

"We can find something that will be acceptable to all concerned, I'm sure." Kimbel reached within an inside pocket of his suit coat and handed Eli Stagg a folded piece of paper:

$500 REWARD FOR THE CAPTURE OF THE KILLERS OF SENATOR WILLARD FRANCIS GRAY. THE RESPONSIBLE PARTIES ARE DESCRIBED AS A DEADLY OUTLAW CALLED BY THE SOBRIQUET "HANDSOME JOHNNY." HIS ACCOMPLICE IS A WOMAN DESCRIBED AS SWEET AND INNOCENT IN LOOKS AND SMALL IN STATURE. HER NAME IS NOT KNOWN. THE PAIR WERE LAST SEEN IN FT. SMITH WHERE THEY SOLD THE MARE THAT SENATOR GRAY WAS RIDING ON HIS FATEFUL DAY. IT IS BELIEVED THAT THE COUPLE ARE ON THEIR WAY TO TEXAS. THE REWARD WILL BE PAID UPON THE CAPTURE AND CONVICTION BY THE STATE OF ARKANSAS.

Above the description were the drawings of a dark-haired man with a black moustache and a woman with a narrow face but attractive features.

The mountain man's features bunched as he read the poster and studied the drawings.

43

"Soon enough," said Kimbel, "I suspect the law will learn their identity. A smart man looking for them would be well advised to keep close company with the marshall's office in Ft. Smith."

Eli Stagg looked up from the paper, his breath souring the air between the two men.

"I reckon I know how to find whatever it is I'm lookin' for, mister."

"Yes. Yes, I suppose you do, Mr. Stagg."

"I'll take that hunnerd dollars now."

He did not bother to count the money. "I take a man at his word," he said. "A bond is a bond. I'll see that your man don't come to trial. You see that the rest of my money's waitin' when the job is done. I ain't a patient man when it comes to collectin' what's due me. You remember that, Mr. Kimbel."

There was a dark warning glowing in the bearish eyes that caused George Kimbel to loosen the knot of his tie.

Chapter Four

Circuit Judge Homer Oliver Price took his seat behind a small claw-foot table borrowed from Mabel Nortrum's boarding house. He rapped the maple gavel on a block of wood so as not to scar Mabel Nortrum's table. The judge's rapping sounded like pistol shots and drew everyone's attention.

Court, as usual, was held in Moody Baker's Gentleman's Club because there never had been a consensus on spending money for a real courthouse, even though the law had long since come to Pecos. At least in the form of Texas Rangers it had.

When Judge Price had hammered the court into session, Moody Baker shouted that the bar was now closed and would be until court was dismissed. A groan went up from the spectators, who were mostly men, but a few women — some of questionable reputation — had also come to the trial, drawn by the dark handsomeness of the man on trial.

The judge appeared frail in his black suit of clothes, but boasted a full mane of snow white hair and shocking blue eyes — an appearance that drew comment from one of the spectators to remark how much he thought the judge looked like Moses.

"How would you have any idea what Moses

looks like?" asked the man sitting next to him.

"I seen a painting of him in a museum in Dallas once."

"You are a damn fool," said the second man, and then each one laughed, but not loud enough to disturb the proceedings.

The judge's voice was deep and resonant and commanding.

"What have you got for me, Ben?"

Texas Ranger Captain Ben Goodlow stood and said, "Your honor, the state of Texas presents for trial, Johnny Montana and Miss Katie Swensen."

"What are they being charged with?" The judge frowned slightly over the indigestion of this morning's breakfast: eggs and chili.

"Well sir, we arrested them for the robbing of the Rawly Bank and Trust, and armed robbery of a pocket watch and twenty cents from one Joe Turner in Wise County. And also, the robbery of a Chinese laundry in Boleweevel of which they took a jarful of Indian head pennies and some clean shirts."

The circuit judge ran a bony stretch of fingers through his snowy hair.

"Did Miss Swensen do any of the actual robbing or is she just considered an accomplice?"

"I don't know, judge," said Captain Goodlow. "I have my suspicions though."

"And what might they be, Captain?"

"I doubt that she ever held a gun on anybody."

"Ma'am," said Judge Price, peering across at

46

Katie Swensen. "Did you help to rob these poor people?"

"I . . . I suppose I did in a way."

"You mean you was along when this feller robbed them?"

"Yes . . . yes sir. I was along."

"This man your husband, is he?"

"No sir."

"He your paramour?"

"I love . . . loved him, yes sir."

The judge sat back in his chair and fell silent for a long full minute. One of the spectators coughed and some heads swiveled around to see who it was.

"Your honor," said Ben Goodlow, breaking the silence. "These folks are also wanted in Arkansas for the killing of a state senator. I have sent wires to the authorities there that we have captured them. They have requested extradition to have these two stand trial in that state."

"Ordinarily, Ben, since they were caught here, they would be tried here for their crimes while in Texas."

"I understand, judge. But, we ought to consider that murder is a worse crime than anything they've done here in Texas and what's fair for everybody ought to be considered."

The hoary head of the judge now turned its attention to Johnny Montana.

"You have any of that money you stole off that farmer or that Chinaman or out of that bank in Rawly, son?"

"Not a penny."

"They have any possessions on them when you caught them, Ben?"

"Just a pair of horses and a fancy pistol that belongs to Senator Gray from Arkansas."

The deep creases and lines in the judge's weathered face looked like where old rivers and arroyos cut through the Texas soil.

"Fellows like you ain't wanted in Texas, son," admonished the judge, fixing his ice blue gaze on the sullen face of Johnny Montana.

"I can't say it has been any sort of pleasure for me neither," said Johnny.

"I'll not tolerate your intemperance in my courtroom. You best hold your tongue!"

The two men locked gazes, but that of the prisoner gave way first. And then Judge Price turned his attention back to Katie Swensen.

"A handsome young woman like you," he said. "Seems to me could have done a lot better in life." He saw the tears sliding down her cheeks and refrained from delivering a sermon to her about the tragedies of travelling the wrong road in life.

"It is the order of this court that the prisoners be remanded in the custody of the Texas Rangers, and that they be returned to the jurisdiction of the state of Arkansas for the purpose of standing trial for their crime in that state. May God and Judge Parker have mercy on your souls." The judge banged his gavel sharply on the block of pine.

Moody Baker shouted that the club was open

48

for business and chairs slid out from under the thirsty as they made their way to the bar.

"Take them back to their cells, Pete," said Ben Goodlow. "I'll make arrangements to begin their transport back to Ft. Smith."

Pete Winter was a tall, youthful ranger who wore his pistol in a cross-draw high on his left hip. He possessed the lanky, handsome, windburned features of Texas men. He was a soft-spoken man whose gaze seemed to take in everything at once.

"Yes sir, Captain." His voice had a polite drawl of a man who had been raised to respect horses, women, and his elders.

He had never witnessed a woman in chains before, and it bothered him now, but he would not allow it to affect his duties as a lawman.

He touched Katie Swensen lightly on the arm in order to direct her to the door. "Ma'am."

Johnny Montana gave him the eye, but the ranger ignored it and nodded with a dip of his head that the outlaw should follow the woman.

The outlaw had to shuffle step because of the irons around his ankles. The chain clanked on the floor as he walked. The judge sipped a whiskey and said to the lawman, "Ben, if those two are found guilty in Judge Parker's court, he will hang them. I'm damn glad it's him and not me that's facing hanging a woman."

"A young woman like that falling so far from grace seems a shame, judge."

"That it does, Ben. That it does."

49

Henry Dollar licked the salt from behind his thumb and then drank down the glass of tequila; its taste was biting. He had ridden to Mobeetie and wired his report to Captain Ben Goodlow at the ranger station in Pecos:

FOUND JIM MCKINNON'S BODY. LOCATED HIS KILLERS IN BIG RIVER. ALL DEAD IN SHOOTOUT. HAVE BEEN ADVISED OF RUSTLING RING OUTSIDE OF TASCOSA. AM GOING THERE NEXT. IN YOUR SERVICE, H. DOLLAR.

Tascosa wasn't much more than a good day's ride. He'd rest part of the day, and head out once the sun dropped beyond the horizon. But right now, he sat on a low bench, leaning his back against the cool adobe wall of a small cantina. He splashed two fingers more of tequila into his glass; it cut the dust out of a man's mouth better than anything he knew of.

The heat of the day like it was, nothing much moved on the lone street of Mobeetie, except the wind. He had left his animal for care and feed at a livery on the south end of the small town. It had been his first task, seeing that his horse was cared for; a man who cared more for himself than his animal was a damn fool.

He closed his eyes and sipped the tequila and thought of other times, better times.

He had left Texas only once; that was to go fight in the War Between the States. He was a rawboned boy full of grit and fight in him, and it seemed the war was one way to let it come out.

The idea of war seemed too glamourous to him.

His daddy had owned a small hardscrabble place up where the wind blew all the while and where the creeks were dry most of the year.

His ma had died early in life, so had two younger brothers. After that, life seemed to get lonelier. And finally, he had grown old enough and the war had come.

He had simply gotten up one morning and saddled his horse and went into the small house where his pa was busy eating his breakfast of corn cakes and sorghum and black coffee.

"I'm joining the war," he had said.

The old man had kept at his meal for a time, chewing with the intensity of a man facing a full day's worth of labor.

"I figure I'll be back in a year, maybe less," he had said to his pa, awaiting some sort of response.

Finally, the old man finished the last corn cake and wiped his mouth, and swallowed some coffee and then said, "I'd go with you if I could."

Then the old man had gotten up and taken down the heavy old Colt's pistol he kept hanging from a peg and handed it to him.

"She fires somewhat to the left and she's heavy as hell, but she'll get the job done."

It was the first gun he had ever killed a man with.

It all seemed so long ago as he sat there sipping the whiskey.

After the war, he had drified west again, through

51

Kansas and the Indian Nations and finally back to Texas and back to the hardscrabble ranch.

The old man had died or drifted away. He found the small ranch abandoned, tumbleweeds blown up against the door, the rooms empty, the corrals empty. Only the wind seemed the same.

The next morning he rode away.

He drifted for a time, picking up odd jobs. But the times were poor and he was just another loose-footed rambler cut loose after the war had ended.

Finally, he did what best suited a man like him, a man that knew horses and how to ride them, that knew guns and how to use them, that knew what it was to be tested by gunfire. He joined the Texas Rangers, D Company in Pecos. That was sixteen years ago and he hadn't regretted it once.

He finished the tequila, stood and stretched and watched the sky turn to crimson as the sun settled beyond the far horizon.

It didn't seem like much to look at, the way it lay flat and endless, but, he knew he would never leave it.

Texas still had the one thing he craved: wildness.

He thought about the troubles he'd be facing in Tascosa as reported to him by the constable at Mobeetie: cow thieves. They were a common lot. Seemed anymore that a man would rather steal a cow than herd one.

Well, he had dealt with them before. Tascosa was just one more place that needed a little law worked on it.

He walked down the street to the livery stable, the loose ring of his spurs trailing behind him, and paid the livery boy six bits for graining and watering his horse.

He put the double rig saddle on the buckskin and mounted.

"Come on, Ike," he said with a light pat to the horse's neck. "Let's clear out before they start playing music over in the cantina, it'll just make me one to loaf around here and watch the señoritas dance. I don't think I can stand the temptation."

Chapter Five

Captain Ben Goodlow arrived at his office before daybreak. The first chore was to set a pot of coffee to brewing on the potbelly; the second, to write a message to be sent by telegraph to the U.S. Marshal's office in Ft. Smith.

He sat at his desk, took a stub pencil in hand and wrote the following: *Have in custody, Johnny Montana and a Miss Katie Swensen, believed to be responsible for the murder of Senator W.F. Gray. Need to make arrangements with your office for the transport and deliverance to your jurisdiction of this couple. I am prepared to deliver them under the authority of a Texas Ranger to some predetermined point of juncture to be handed over to a Federal officer from your district. Please advise as to your providing such an officer and as to where and when. Respectfully, Captain Ben Goodlow, Texas Ranger Station, Pecos.*

The lawman reread the message and then laid the stub pencil down and checked the coffee. The warm rich smell had permeated the room. The coffee not quite ready, the captain walked the message over to the telegraph office and handed it to the telegrapher, a man named Sparks.

"Send this now, Charley," he said.

"Billed to your office, Cap?"

"Bill it to my office," said the ranger. "I want you to bring me the answer as soon as one arrives — don't dawdle, Charley."

54

"Oh, no sir, Cap. Sending them two back to Arkansas to be hanged, huh?"

"Sending them back, whether or not they're hanged is up to the state of Arkansas."

"She's a terrible good-looking woman, Cap. I can't imagine no judge ordering a rope put around her neck."

Without further comment, the lawman turned and walked back toward his office. He thought about the woman standing before Judge Parker's court — The Hanging Judge — and wondered what the outcome would be. He doubted that even Parker would hang a woman. He hated to think that he might.

Pete Winter was waiting for his boss when Ben Goodlow reached his office; the young ranger was also an early riser. He stood there by the potbelly, blowing the steam off a tin cup of hot coffee.

"Pete," greeted the captain as he shut the door behind him.

"Captain."

"I just sent a wire to Ft. Smith regarding the transport of the two prisoners back to the authorities there. I should be hearing soon as to how we're going to arrange things."

Pete remained silent while he sipped at his coffee. He, like most men of his cut, was not a great talker. Whatever ideas he had on a matter, he kept to himself.

Ben Goodlow had raised Pete Winter. He and his wife, Frieda. To be sure it had been an odd circumstance the way that Joe Winter had simply rode to their ranch one day with young Pete in hand and said that since his wife had died, he could no longer raise the boy. Ben had known Joe for a long time. There never was a question about taking over the responsibility. Pete came to be like their own.

He was proud of what he saw now, standing and sipping coffee. Aside from what he could teach the boy about horses, guns, and men, Pete Winter seemed to possess all the natural instincts and abilities that a fighting lawman needed.

To the Captain's way of thinking, Texas Rangers were a special breed of men. It took more than just carrying a gun and a badge and arresting hardcases. He had always warned his boys, "Most of the men you will go after have a lot more mean in them than you do, but mean don't make a man tough."

He also taught them such matters as never abusing their horses or their prisoners. "Any man that does," he warned, "will not get along with me."

As a Texas Ranger, Pete Winter fit the bill just fine in the captain's mind. The sandy-haired boy had grown into a fine young man — tall and handsome, polite as a parson, and tough as a mustang.

Pete Winter was the youngest ranger in the company, but time and again, he proved to be one of the finest, most resourceful lawmen the captain had ever known. He trusted the young ranger completely.

Ben Goodlow drank the hot as hell coffee and removed the battered Stetson from his head.

"Pete, I have requested that the Marshal's office in Ft. Smith send us one of their men — at least partways — to meet us and take charge of the prisoners."

"Makes good sense, Captain."

"Trouble is, the Federal Marshals are so over-burdened, it ain't likely that anyone will be sent all the way to Pecos to escort those two — not for some time anyway. It's why I volunteered that we'd escort them to some halfway point, hoping that would expedite the matter. I'd like to wash my hands of this business as soon as can be done."

"How many men you plan on sending as an escort, Captain?"

"Just one, Pete — can't spare more, and even if I could, I figure one ought to be plenty."

"I reckon you'd want Henry Dollar for the job," pouring a second cup of coffee.

"Henry's the most seasoned man of the outfit, but Henry's up in Mobeetie, got a wire from him yesterday. He found Jim McKinnon's body. . . ."

Both men lapsed into a moment of respectful silence.

"Anyway, Henry's on his way to Tascosa, seems there's a rustling ring operating over that way. He won't be back for a couple of weeks. I want to send you as escort for the prisoners, Pete."

The young lawman shifted his weight as the only indication of what the captain had just said.

"Well, Ben, you know I will if that's what you've decided."

"Don't let this job fool you, son. Travelling over

57

most of the country you'll have to cross can be dangerous at best, carrying along two prisoners makes it even more so. Most of that land is desolate, without water. It's a bad country all around. There's still some renegade bands of Comanche roaming around out there and hardcases the law ain't caught up with yet. Any one of them can kill you and will if given the chance."

"I'll stay cautious, Cap'n. When should I prepare to leave?"

"As soon as I get word back from Ft. Smith. You go ahead and get your possibles ready, go down to the livery and pick out a pair of riding horses and a pack mule to carry your provisions with. Get supplied over to the trading post — I figure two weeks' worth ought to do it. Be ready when I get word."

Pete Winter adjusted his sweat-stained Stetson so that it touched the tops of his ears and drank the last dregs of his coffee cup.

"I'll get 'er done, Cap'n, you just yell out when you're ready for me to start."

Ben Goodlow watched his protégé step through the door, cross the street, and head for the livery. The boy was chock full of belief in himself, exactly what the older lawman knew he would need for such a journey.

Having worn the badge for as long as he had, Ben Goodlow knew that whenever a job enforcing the law looked easy, it usually wasn't — too many good lawman had died believing otherwise.

He thought briefly about assigning another

ranger to the escort, but let the thought pass without giving much credence to it. If the boy was big enough to wear the badge, he was big enough to do the job.

Eli Stagg dismounted his mule in front of the U.S. Marshal's office in Ft. Smith, Arkansas.

The lawman at the desk lifted his gaze in time to see the grizzled countenance of a man who smelled like campfire smoke and grease glaring down at him. The effect was unnerving.

"Some way I can help you, mister?"

The hunter reached inside his shirt and pulled out a crumpled piece of paper.

"I seed this poster over in Mud Bottom," he said, spreading it atop the deputy's desk, tapping a thick finger down on it.

"It's for them two that killed that politician. I aim to claim it."

"You're too late, mister. They've already been captured. I got word in this morning."

The big man grunted his seemingly disappointment.

"Where?"

"Over in Texas. It's where they all head to sooner or later."

"Well then, I reckon I done made myself a trip fer nothin'."

"I reckon so."

The lawman watched the big man shift the weight of the Creedmore rifle in his hand.

"Texas, you say?"

Caleb Drew nodded his head.

"Well, reckon I'm just wastin' good time standin' here." Then, he turned and walked out of the office.

Joe Duty, a deputy who had been sitting at another desk with his right foot bandaged and propped on a chair, leaned and spat tobacco juice into a tin can.

"Big as a damn tree that son of a gun was, Caleb. Smelled like a sackful of dead squirrels."

"Takes all kinds, I guess."

"Bounty hunter?"

"Looks as though he was."

"What're you planning on doing about those folks the rangers are holding?"

It was a good question. He was short on men and long on assignments. Crime had gotten to be a popular thing, and Judge Parker was holding court every day and still, nobody could seem to keep up. Right at the moment, aside from himself, he had two deputies: Joe Duty, who had been shot in the foot the previous week by a drunken whore, and Al Freemont.

"Well, unless you figure you can ride with that foot of yours, the only man I have left is Al Freemont."

"Reckon ol' Al ain't going to be too happy about that," said Joe Duty, lining up the can to spit again.

"Al's getting long in the tooth and as grumpy as an old maid, that's for certain."

The old lawman had been around for years, complained about his arthritis every time he climbed

60

down out of the saddle, complained about the gout in his big toe whenever it rained, complained about his eyesight. Caleb Drew had been patient with him, out of respect for the service he had given the U.S. Marshal's office over the years. Besides, he had been a personal favorite of Judge Parker's.

"Well, I guess you don't have much choice, Caleb. But I'm glad it's you telling him and not me."

Caleb Drew rose from his chair, lifted his low-crowned hat from a peg and said, "Watch the store."

He walked the three blocks to the telegraph office. Hiram Bisby was swatting flies when he entered. He handed the clerk a note and said, "Send it."

Hiram read the note before sitting down to his telegrapher's key.

The clerk looked up through his thick wire-rimmed glasses.

"You sending Al Freemont all the way to the Indian Nations?"

"I didn't come here to seek your counsel on what my job should be, Hiram, just send the damn telegram."

"Yes sir, marshal, you say so."

The man standing across the street, a Creedmore rifle cradled in his arms, was unnoticed.

Al Freemont wasn't feeling so good when U.S. Marshal Caleb Drew found him in his room at the Ozark Hotel.

"I need you to ride to the Nations, Al. Need you to meet a Texas Ranger there and take charge of two prisoners and escort them back to Ft. Smith." The message was straightforward and simple, but Al Freemont looked at his boss as if he were talking donkey talk.

"That's a ride and then some, Caleb." Al Freemont had the thinness of a man suffering from the consumption: his rheumy-eyed face was lined with creases and possessed the sad, long look of a hound.

"I know how far the Nations are. You're the only man available, Al. I wouldn't send you if you wasn't." Caleb Drew could see it was not going to be easy. The old lawman laying on his bed crosswise had once been a good man, but age and booze had dulled him.

"I . . . I don't know if I can," pleaded the deputy. "The gout's pulling on my big toe like a beaver chewing it off."

"It's what you get paid to do, Al. Things like this is your job."

The old lawman cradled his head in his hands, the marshal could smell the stale breath of booze.

"Look at yourself, Al. Look what you've let yourself become. Hell, you used to be one of the finest lawmen anywhere."

Al Freemont simply looked up at him. Caleb Drew could see that this wasn't going to work, could see that the old man wasn't up to the task. He felt badly that he had even come to ask.

"Ah, to hell with it, Al. Go on back to your

rest. I'm sorry I bothered you." He reached for the door knob.

The deputy coughed hard, struggled upright. "Hold on, Caleb. I'll go. Just give me a little time . . . you know, to sorta get my sand packed down."

"Sure, Al. You come around to see me when you're ready," said the lawman, unsure as to whether he had made the right choice.

"Caleb?"

"What, Al?"

"I don't know what happened to me, except I got old and things started breaking down on the inside. Maybe the ride will do me good."

Drew made a weak effort at a smile.

The old lawman coughed again and wiped the side of his mouth with the back of his hand as though waiting for a reprieve.

"You don't need to prove anything to me, Al."

"It ain't for you," said the deputy. "It's for me."

Ben Goodlow received the telegram from U.S. Marshal Caleb Drew of Fort Smith while he was eating his breakfast. The telegram stated that a deputy U.S. marshal by the name of Al Freemont would meet the ranger and his prisoners at Ardmore in the Indian Nations, that it was the extent of what the Federal lawman could offer in the way of assistance. It was more than Ben Goodlow had expected. He'd take it. He summoned Pete Winter.

"How close are you to being ready, Pete?"

"Well sir, I'm waiting for my order to be filled

over at the outpost, and the riding horses to be shod. I'd say within the next hour or two."

"I'll draw some funds for travelling money from the bank for you, son. You meet me at the office when you are prepared to go."

By ten that morning, Pete Winter led two riding horses and a pack mule full of supplies up to the Ranger Headquarters and tied them to the hitch rail.

Stepping inside, he placed a package wrapped in brown paper on the captain's desk: "Riding clothes for Miss Swensen," he said.

Ben Goodlow took the package back to the cells and left them with the woman to get dressed in; he brought Johnny Montana forth to the office while she did so.

While they were waiting for Katie Swensen to change, the captain turned to Pete and said, "Don't let your guard down out there, son. There's a thousand things that could go wrong."

The young ranger grinned embarrassedly. "I will, Cap'n."

"Here's a map of the territory from here to the Nations," said the older lawman, handing Pete a rolled parchment.

"Thanks, Cap'n," said Pete, tucking the map into the saddlebags he carried. "I've been up that way a time or two before, I've marked where I believe water holes to be."

Katie Swensen made her appearance from the cell area. She was dressed in a dark blue woolen shirt, corduroy pants, and low-heeled boots.

"Young lady," said the lawman, "If you promise not to cause this officer a fuss during your journey, I'll forego the handcuffs at this time for your comfort."

"Thank you," she said, her voice barely audible.

"You are welcome, but I'm instructing Pete, here, to let you wear iron all the way to the Nations if necessary. He won't tolerate any misbehavior on your part, do you understand?"

She nodded her head.

"You wire in when you get there, Pete," were the last instructions he knew to give.

He watched the trio ride out, taking the north road. Another time, another place, they could have been simply three young folks riding out for a picnic.

Something uncertain nagged at his gut. He would have felt less troubled had Henry Dollar been the one running the show. But then, he told himself, his uneasiness was more a personal matter than a practical one: Pete was like his own son.

Chapter Six

Al Freemont had been a day's ride out of Ft. Smith, had crossed over into the Indian Nations, and had the deep sense that someone was dogging his trail. He stopped several times and waited, spelling his mount and his sore backside, but no one came up the trail behind him.

It was a hard business, riding all day; a business better suited for younger men.

The sipping whiskey he nibbled at every few miles seemed to take some of the ache out, but not enough to keep him from being miserable.

Damned if he knew why he had let Caleb Drew shame him into taking this journey. *Foolish pride,* he told himself. *A man shouldn't have more pride than he can carry.*

He let his mind drift back to other times, earlier times, in order to ignore his present discomfort. He remembered the glory days when the law was less complicated than it was now. If a man threw down on you, you shot him, and that was the end of it. Now, you was expected to bring a man in for trial, for judges and attorneys and juries to decide. All a lawman was, it seemed to Al Freemont as he rode along the uneven trail, was some sort of escort, a paper server.

The whiskey eased his pain but not his mind. *Sure in hell there was somebody back there.*

New Orleans proved to be hot and humid with the warm moist winds blowing up from the Gulf. Things moved slow: people, horses, stray dogs, time.

Lowell Biggs spent most of his ride down the main street, into a section called the French Quarter, swiveling his head in an effort to take in all the sights. The traffic of carriages and wagons and riders on horseback was heavy, the sidewalks full of pedestrians.

From wrought-iron balconies, coffee-colored women shouted to them in French and blew kisses down on them. Dark-eyed men stood in doorways or leaned against lampposts and studied their movement.

"Damn," said Lowell Biggs to his brother. "You ever seen such a place as this?"

"I don't need to have seen it to know what it is," said Carter, keeping his gaze directly ahead of him.

"What do you suppose those gals up there are saying to us?"

"Mind to our own business, Lowell. They're just whores that have a funny way of speaking is all. We don't have time for consortin'. Texas is still a long way off and that's where we aim to be."

"Well maybe they are whores, Carter. But, I ain't never seen any women in Autauga County to compare with them — not by a damn sight, I ain't."

"Keep your eyes stuck in your head, little brother," ordered Carter. "The onliest thing we need in this town are supplies. It's so hot and muggy it feels like someone dropped a warsh cloth over my face!"

A shrill whistle from above, from one of the balconies, drew Lowell's attention. The woman that leaned over the railing smiled broadly and swished her hips.

Unlike most of the others, this one's skin was the color of milk, her hair black as a raven's feathers.

"Allo mon doux, hello my sweet. Come and visit Danielle, eh. I show you a good time, yes?"

He was struck with her exotic beauty. She was wearing very little, and she leaned forward across the railing in order to show him even more of herself.

He removed his hat from his head and held it over his heart. She wiggled a finger at him to come.

"Venir chere, come my darling, I will give you much plaisir, mon doux."

Carter's face twisted grim the minute he realized that Lowell had halted his progress, had been engaged by one of the whores. He wheeled his dun around and walked it back to where his little brother sat in the middle of the street looking up at the balcony tart.

"Lowell! I warned you, we ain't got time for this!"

"Why the hell not?" said Lowell, irritated at his brother for having broken the spell she had been casting upon him.

"I already told you why! We're on our way to Texas to find that bastard Johnny Montana!"

"Well, it ain't like Texas is exactly right around the corner, now is it? What's an hour more going to make in the difference? You may be older, Carter, but I'm a grown man and I can make my own decisions. And right now I'm deciding to go on up and see that lady." His grin was spread from ear to ear as he looked up at the woman who was being even more explicit with him, more daring.

Carter cast a furtive glance up at the woman. She had pulled her bodice down and exposed her breasts.

"You like what you see, chere?"

Carter saw that other women on the balconies were acting just as lewd now that they had drawn the attention of the two men below them.

"Look at 'em all, Carter!" said Lowell, thoroughly absorbed by the lascivious behavior of the women.

Carter could see that short of putting a pistol to his brother's head, that he wasn't going to deter the younger man's desire or his interest in the chalky-skinned woman who stood practically naked on the balcony.

"Alright! You go on an get it over with, Lowell. But, I'm givin' you just thirty minutes to get your business taken care of. I'll go and see if they sell anything in this town besides *playsure;* things we *need,* like beans and flour and coffee. Come tomorrow morning, you'll be damned glad one of us kept our attention to the matters at hand!"

"Fine, Carter, you go and take care of that stuff, I'll be waitin' when you get back." Lowell hardly noticed or cared where his brother rode off to.

He walked his horse over to a black iron hitch post shaped in the form of a horse's head, dismounted and tied up.

An ornate wrought-iron gate gave entrance to a cobblestone courtyard that he figured would allow him access to the building itself.

The courtyard contained a small pond that had gold fish in it and a stone cherub holding a pitcher from which water poured. Also in the courtyard were trees with moss hanging from their branches; the smell of dampness hung in the air.

Lowell found a set of stairs, some weak with rot, leading up the side of the building where the woman was. He was careful in climbing.

She was waiting for him, standing there in the doorway.

As he drew near, he could smell the sweet scent of lilac, could see the perspiration of her skin, the blackness of her hair.

She had large dark eyes that tracked his movements.

"So, you have come to see Danielle, eh, come to taste her charms." Her speech was strange, exotic, haunting.

"If that's you, darlin', then you're what I come here for."

"Come in, chere," she offered, stepping aside

to allow him to enter.

He removed his hat and knocked some of the dust from his clothes before sidling past her.

His heartbeat increased.

The room was large and open. He could see where the shuttered doors opened unto the balcony. White limp curtains hung from the open windows. A brass bed was shoved against one wall, an armoire against another; a steamer trunk with worn leather straps sat at the foot of the bed.

The room was silent and warm. Pewter sunlight filtered through the open windows and fell across the bare board floor.

She reached for him, reached for the buttons of his shirt.

"Come, lay on the bed, chere," she whispered. He found himself becoming lost within her beauty, within the sweetness of her kisses. Time itself became lost.

"Lowell!" He heard his name being called from a distance.

"Lowell!"

He realized that he had dozed, had been lulled by the warmth of the room. He shook off his drowsiness and moved to the balcony forgetting for the moment that he was naked.

"Goddamn it, Lowell! Put your clothes on and let's go!"

Carter shifted restlessly in his saddle directly below him, a large grain sack of supplies tied to his saddle horn, his countenance grim.

"You don't get down here this minute, boy, I'll

leave you here — I damn well mean it!"

It seemed like no time at all had passed since he first climbed the stairs. He turned, looked sheepishly at the woman sitting on the bed. She smoked a black cheroot. He thought to himself that he could stay here with her forever.

"Sorry, Danielle . . . that's Carter down there . . . I promised I'd be but half an hour . . ."

She gave him a wan smile but showed no particular interest.

He sat on the side of the bed, dressing as best he could, wanting to hurry, wanting not to.

He had only known one other woman in a carnal way — a neighbor's daughter back in Autauga County. But, the girl had been fat and homely and buck-toothed and hadn't known dip about pleasing a man. Lowell figured that the neighbor girl didn't count.

"Me and Carter's got business to take care of, got to go to Texas. But I'm thinking that as soon as it's over with, I'd like to sorta come back this way . . ." He fell silent, hopeful that she would be happy over the announcement. Instead, she seemed impatient, moving off the bed toward the balcony, glancing down at the waiting brother, moving back into the room.

"Your friend, he is waiting for you," she said, blowing smoke rings toward the ceiling.

"Well anyways," he said, pulling on his last boot, "I can't say's I've ever known anyone like you . . . you sure are some kind of female."

She moved to the door and held it open for him.

72

"I never knowed a woman that smoked seegars before," he said as a final effort to be charming. He kissed her on the cheek.

She closed her eyes and said, "You better go, chere."

He heard the door close behind him with a sad finality as he descended the stairs.

Carter's face was flushed with anger and impatience at having had to wait for him.

"I hope you got everything out of your system, Lowell. 'Cause we ain't stopping to dally anymore!"

They rode west out of town, rode until the air rising up from the nearby bayous turned dank and mysterious. Great white herons flew up out of swamps that were bordered by stands of moss laden cypress. There were snakes and alligators and death lying within those swamps. Carter found everything about this country to be strange and offensive.

They rode for a time in silence, the blaze of sun warm upon their faces.

"Well, little brother, how much did that little romp back there cost you?"

Lowell had been lost in thought, the image of the white-skinned woman floating in his mind. The question broke him from his reverie.

"What do you mean?"

"I mean, how much did you have to pay her?"

Lowell's features went from dreamy to confused. He let the question rest in his mind for a long full moment. Then, it dawned on him, and with a great deal of glee, he answered: "She didn't charge me anything, big brother. Didn't ask for one red cent. I guess maybe she just favored the way I looked."

Carter suddenly pulled back on the reins of his mount.

"Lowell, you are as green as spring tomatoes. Women like that don't just give themselves away. Now how much of our money was it that you spent?"

"Honest, Carter. She never even mentioned money . . ."

"Check your pockets you dern fool!"

Something heavy passed through Lowell's mood as he felt through his empty pockets.

"Damn!" he muttered. "My roll's gone!"

"How'd you let her get at it in the first place?"

"Don't know . . . except . . . it seems I might have dozed off for a spell."

"That's all it took. She rolled you blind. Come on!" shouted Carter, wheeling his dun back around toward the town.

"Ah, Carter . . ." But before the younger brother could protest, the older one had already begun to spur his mount into a trot.

By the time the pair reached the edge of the city, the sky had turned a dusty rose in the descending darkness. Gas lights flickered along the street casting tongues of light onto the wet cobblestones. Twenty minutes earlier, there had been a brief thunderstorm that had left them soaked, the brims of their hats down over their faces. Now, the heavy air had the added smell of spices emanating from the many open windows where Cajun food was being prepared.

"Cursed place," complained Carter. "Nothing but wet and smelly and full of evilness."

Shadowy figures moved along the boardwalks. The cry of prostitutes still rang down from the balconies, from the darkened doorways, their numbers increased with the coming of nightfall.

They reined up in front of the tall house with the wrought iron gate leading to the courtyard. Lowell looked up at the now empty balcony. A stain of yellow light fell on the frame of windows.

"She may not be there, Carter. What'll we do if she ain't?"

"We'll worry about that when the time comes. Let's go." Lowell saw his brother shift the revolver on his hip and then dismount.

"What do you plan to do, Carter?"

"I'm planning on getting a damn fool's money back," he said as he pushed open the iron gate and stepped into the courtyard. "You comin'?"

Lowell slid out of his saddle and hurried to catch up.

The heels of their boots, in spite of their effort to move quietly, knocked on the cobblestones.

"Be careful of them steps, Carter, some of them's rotted."

The first step wasn't rotted, but it groaned under Carter's bulk. He pulled his pistol and continued to climb.

It seemed like an eternity to Lowell before they

reached the top of the stairs. Pausing, Carter leaned his ear to the door.

He could hear laughter inside — a man's and a woman's laughter. He turned and whispered in a hoarse breath: "They're here, Lowell. You had better pull your piece."

"Carter . . ." Lowell's voice broke with apprehension. "Carter, it ain't hardly worth it, shooting someone over money. It wasn't all that much . . . not more than seventy dollars."

"Shut your yap!" demanded the older brother through clenched teeth. The laughter in the room suddenly stopped. For a long moment, silence shrouded the house — inside and out. A mist of fog was beginning to claim the land and its buildings.

"Who's out there?" demanded a man's voice from within the room.

"I come to see the lady!" shouted Carter.

"The lady is bizee. Come back tomorrow, eh?" came the thickly accented voice from within.

Carter stepped back just far enough to raise a heavy boot and brought it hard against the door, rattling it nearly off its hinges; a second kick knocked it open.

Lowell and Carter Biggs found themselves facing a naked couple entwined on the bed.

"I guess she's home," said Carter, sarcastically to his brother.

The man on the bed cried out, as though he had been wounded. He scrambled to retrieve some respectability among the bedding. A second movement coming through the door behind them drew everyone's attention.

Framed there in the busted doorway stood a lithe, little man with dark slick hair, hawkish nose, and dressed like a dandy clear down to the powder gray spats he wore.

"You have interrupted my bezniss, mon ami," he said, pointing a nickel-plated derringer at them.

The man on the bed leapt to his feet with a scream.

"What is the meaning of this — am I being robbed?"

Carter shifted his gaze from the dandy to the naked man.

"You are," he said to the frightened toad. "But not by us — by him! You ain't the first chicken to get plucked by these two today!"

The man dropped to his knees upon the bed. Bringing his hands together in prayerful gesture, he pleaded: "Please . . . I only come for a leetle plaisir . . . I beg you not to shoot me, monsieur!"

The man's demonstrative plea was just enough to divert the attention of the gunman.

Carter snapped his arm straight upwards and in the same instant pulled the trigger on the revolver he had been holding in his hand. The explosion rocked the room. The bullet struck the dandy high in the chest, slightly right of center, and knocked him backwards against the door jamb. The derringer clattered to the floor.

The naked man flounced on the bed, his every sound a wail, a plea for mercy. "Oh please . . .

please, mon ami . . . do not kill me also!"

The woman had sprung from the bed like a panther. Her own screams joining those of the hysterical paramour. Too late Carter saw the dirk clutched in her hand. Lowell, who stood still staring at the dying man, felt something like the blow of a fist strike him between the shoulder blades.

The knife plunged in to the hilt, the blade breaking off into bone.

Carter swung the barrel of the pistol around. For one brief second, the woman stared into the large black hole of the barrel.

The second explosion sounded louder than the first. The bullet tore a neat hole through the woman's forehead and flung her backwards onto the bed. Her blood covered the naked man, causing him to topple over into a faint.

A movement by the door caused Carter's attention to be drawn there again. The dandy was still alive, still trying to crawl further into the room.

Carter felt the sliding tug of his brother as Lowell dropped to his knees, his breath labored.

"Carter, what's happened to me?" His eyes were searching those of his sibling for an answer.

"Come on, little brother. We've got to get the hell out of here!" Carter, using his full strength, lifted Lowell to his feet. When he did so, he felt the warm stickiness of Lowell's life blood spill over his hands.

Carter stared into the ashen face of his only kin and wondered if he would even make it out of the room alive. With the mighty bulk of one arm, he practically carried the wounded man toward the doorway.

The dandy had gotten as far as balancing himself on his hands and knees. Carter paused long enough to pat the pockets of the man's jacket and vest. Feeling a lump, he reached into a vest pocket and retrieved a handful of paper money.

The dandy's eyes cowered within his pained face.

As a final angry gesture, Carter pushed the man over with his boot. "I guess your robbing days are over," he said, continuing to carry Lowell toward the doorway.

It was a chore trying to get the wounded brother down the rickety steps. Lowell's legs had lost their steadiness.

By the time they had made the courtyard and come through the iron gate, a crowd had gathered in front of the building, their interest drawn by the sound of gunfire.

Carter, half-carrying his wounded brother like a scarecrow, pushed his way through the on-lookers. Someone said: "Look, that fellow's bleeding like a stuck hog!"

And it was true. Lowell's blood was splattering on the wet cobblestones in jagged, crimson patterns.

They reached the horses, and, with one great effort, Carter flung the wounded brother into the saddle.

"Hold on tight, Lowell."

"It feels like my back is set afire," groaned Lowell as he slumped forward in the saddle, feeling the horn press into his gut.

Carter made his own saddle and, gripping the reins of Lowell's horse in one hand, he drove his heels into the flanks of the dun, spiriting the powerful animal into a dead run.

Lowell's hat went flying; he could feel the warm fluid of blood draining down his spine, soaking his trousers. A numbness was setting in. He felt the wind against his fevered face. The yellow flames of the gas lights suddenly disappeared behind them and into the darkness they rode.

Chapter Seven

Tascosa, Texas

Royal Curtiss was busy staining the front of his shirt with the grease drippings from a fried chicken; a pile of gristly bones lay piled on a plate in front of him. Next to that, a stein of beer. The leg of the chicken was the last of it, a big fryer that Maybelle had delivered him for his lunch.

He was working down into the double bone of the chicken leg with his teeth when the door to his office rattled open.

"You City Marshal Curtiss?" asked the big man standing in the frame of the door. Wind blew in behind him and upset a stack of papers on the chicken eater's desk.

"You mind closing that?" said the man over a mouthful of bone, his lips and chin greasy.

Henry Dollar closed the door behind him and stepped farther into the room. What he saw was the slovenly man sitting behind his desk, a plate of chicken bones, and a pair of protruding, suspicious eyes.

"Yeah, I'm the city marshal," said the chicken eater. "Who's asking?"

"Name's Henry Dollar, Texas Ranger."

"Didn't know there was any rangers in the area," said the man behind the desk, teasing the last sprig of meat from the chicken leg and then dropping it on top of the others.

Henry watched as the man wiped his greasy fingers on the cracked leather vest he wore. A brass badge was pinned to the vest.

"I got word that there was some trouble up around here," said Henry, not liking the man all that much. "Was over in Mobeetie on some business when I was told about a rustling problem. Decided to have a look into it."

The rotund lawman placed both hands on the edge of his desk and pushed himself back in his chair. His mouth gnarled up into a stupid grin.

"Well hell, that must have been some story to get 'em to send a ranger over here." The man's grin turned sour.

"Where the hell are you rangers when I got drunks to corral at night, or wild cowboys who like to shoot their pistols off at anything that moves?"

"I rode over here to help put an end to your situation, mister," warned Henry, "not to be abused by you."

"Wal, maybe you ought to just get back on your horse and ride out again — we don't need no strangers coming in and dictating how things is going to be."

Henry stepped close to the man's desk, and bent slightly at the waist before speaking.

"You're walking awful close to a line you don't want to cross with me, marshal. I didn't ride here for nothing, and I'm not riding out for nothing. I came here to do a job, and I plan to see it through. You don't want to cooperate, you stay the hell clear. You get in my way, try to interfere, you'll pay a hard price."

City Marshal Royal Curtiss stared into the eyes of the big man, saw no promise of anything good, saw no cause to challenge this man.

The color drained from the chicken-eater's face.

"Okay . . . go ahead and do your investigatin' . . . nose around . . . who cares."

"Fine. Now take a pencil and write down the names of the nearest ranchers around here and directions on how to reach their spreads."

Henry waited until the city marshal had completed the list and then took his leave of the squat useless man.

The first name on the list was a man named Clave Miller. His was the nearest place on the list as well: three miles west of town, first road to the left.

Out upon the open grassy plain, he saw a herd of cattle grazing, their white faces and reddish brown hides moving slowly. Their long horns rose and dipped as they lifted their heads to watch the rider pass by and then resumed their graze.

A mile or so down the wagon trace he had taken off the main road, he saw in the distance a windmill, its blades spinning in the wind, saw too the metal roofs of several small buildings.

He spurred the buckskin to a dog trot until he came within shouting distance of the main house, a house that needed a painting.

"Hallo inside," he called out. It didn't pay to

just walk up to a man's door and knock, not in this country it didn't.

There was a long slow moment of silence before the door opened and a woman stepped into its framework. The wind billowed the bottom of her dress. She put one hand to her brow to shade her eyes.

"What do you want here, mister?" The question rang strong and clear.

"My name's Dollar. I'm with the Texas Rangers. Came to see your man. Clave Miller, if he *is* your man?"

"What'd he do?"

"Nothing I know about."

"Then why you here to see him?"

"Looking into cattle rustling hereabouts. Wanted to see if he had been a victim of said crimes."

"Rustling ain't nothing new in these parts, mister. Rustling's been going on for years. How come you to just now be showing up?"

"Just now heard, sister."

She dropped the hand down away from her face. She had a stark face, hair pulled back tight, plain and unattractive — much like the land itself.

"Might as well step down, Mr. Dollar. Come on up to the house. Water your horse over there at the tank if you want. It's a hot day all around."

He loosened the cinch on Ike's saddle and lifted it up from his back for a few seconds allowing air to pass between horse and blanket, after which he led him to the water tank and let him drink.

84

He scouted the layout of the place as he did so. A few buildings, a couple of corrals with good-looking horses in them, a chicken coop. Not a bad spread.

He removed his Stetson and dipped a hand down in the water, bringing up enough to splash on his face and neck and head.

Turning back to the house where the woman still stood in the doorway, he gave idle thought to what it would be like to have his own spread, a few hundred cattle; quiet, steady work laid before him that did not call for dealing with bandits, horse thieves, rustlers or killers. It was difficult to imagine.

There was still no sign of a man around the place.

He stopped within easy distance of the woman. She had the stark suspicious gaze of a woman alone on the plains.

"Your husband, is he about, ma'am?"

"He's off checking the herds, him and the other hands."

"You reckon when he might be back?"

"Hard saying. Depends on where the cattle are at."

The lawman stood staring out at the vast flat sweep of land, at the long straight horizon where the faded blue sky and the brown earth were seamed together. He stood there listening to the wind, and listening to the silence that was left whenever the wind stopped.

"You hungry mister?"

He was. Hungry and near wore out after a ride that had begun before sunup.

"Yes, ma'am. I surely am."

"Then come on in the house, wipe your feet if you don't mind."

He scraped the soles of his boots on the bottom of the door frame and stepped inside.

The warm scent of fresh baked bread caused his hunger to instantly increase. She pointed to one of the four chairs around a square, scarred oak table that would have taken two men to lift.

He hung his Stetson on the back of the chair and sat down.

She glanced disapprovingly at his spurs. He started to remove them.

"No, that's okay," she said. "Do you drink tea, Mr. Dollar?" He didn't, normally.

"Yes ma'am, tea is fine."

"Good. It's hard to find a man that drinks tea. Hard to find anybody that drinks tea out here." She sat a copper tea kettle on a big iron stove that had ornate nickel plating along its edges and porcelain handles. Several fresh-baked loaves of bread sat in pans along the window sill.

He studied her as she prepared the tea, taking it from a tin can and placing the leaves into a small metal basket: A large woman. Raw-boned hands, reddened knuckles. The hair, brown and faded, streaks of silver. The eyes, tired.

It seemed a great effort to do so, but when she turned to bring him the tea in a china cup, she smiled. The lines around her mouth creased

86

deeply — Texas sun was no good for a woman's skin.

She took one of the loaves of bread out of a pan and cut it in two. She reached on a shelf and took down a jar of apricot preserves. She laid both in front of him. A pot of stew was simmering on the stove. She ladled him a tin plate full and put that in front of him as well. He thought for a moment that he might faint from hunger.

"You go ahead and eat, I already have earlier," she said.

She sat across from him and drank her tea while he did his best to restrain himself from simply shoveling the food in as fast as he could.

"You are a handsome man," she said after several long minutes of watching him eat.

He was not sure what to say to such a comment.

"How about some more?" she said when he finished sopping the last of the stew's gravy from the plate with the partial loaf of bread he held onto the whole time.

He nodded his head and remained silent.

The second plate tasted as good as the first and was chasing all the hungry wolves out of the cellar of his stomach.

"Where'd you say you come from?" she asked.

He swallowed a potato and said: "Originally from Pecos, but most lately from Mobeetie."

"You have law business over there as well?"

"Not there exactly — but over in Big River."

"Mobeetie ain't much of a town," she said, renewing the tea in her cup. "Bought a dress there once. It was a pretty dress."

He wasn't sure if she was speaking directly to him or not; her eyes were looking up at the ceiling when she spoke.

"Clave, he likes to ride over to Mobeetie now and again. They got the only cathouse in this part of the Panhandle," she said. "You know how men can be, Mr. Dollar."

"No ma'am."

"Well, they can be plum awful sometimes. Would you like some more tea? I've got plenty."

"No ma'am. I sort of hoped your husband would have come in by now. I think I need to talk to him about this rustling business around here."

She shrugged and cupped her chin in the palm of her hand and stared at him until he dropped his eyes down to his empty plate.

"You married, Mr. Dollar?"

"No ma'am."

"Ever been?"

"No ma'am."

She sighed, stood, and went to a basin near the window. He watched as her shoulders rose and then dropped again in deep sigh as she stood there staring out the window.

"Being married can sometimes be hard," she said. "Living out here in the middle of nowhere, listening to the wind blow all the time, hearing the bawl of cattle can be hard. It makes me cry sometimes, Mr. Dollar."

He could understand her loneliness. The frontier

was a rugged place for women.

She turned and faced him.

"Do you think me an attractive woman, Mr. Dollar?"

The question caught him off guard.

"Well, ma'am. I guess I shouldn't be the one to judge," he said.

"Why not? You're a man. Surely you can see for yourself whether or not a man would find me interesting to look at."

"I would say that most men would find your looks to be agreeable," he said. In a way, he had not lied to her. Even though plain and somewhat large as females went, with a little fixing and a little care, he could see where she could draw a man's attention to her.

"You are a kind person for having said so," she replied. "Would you like more to eat?"

"No ma'am. I reckon I'd best be going," he said, the poor light in the room indicated that the sun was sagging in the west.

"Then how about a cup of coffee before you go? I can see that you are not a fancier of tea," she said, glancing at his half empty cup, "but it was kind of you anyway. Coffee won't take but a minute. If you like you can smoke outside while I make it?"

He knew that she was holding on to his company, not wanting to be left alone. Well, maybe if he lingered a bit, her man would show. He could see no harm in a few more minutes.

He stepped out into the long shadows of the

house, shadows cast by a setting sun. The wind had died, the windmill stood silent and still. He pulled his makings and rolled a cigarette and struck a match off the heel of his boot.

He thought about the woman inside, thought about her loneliness, about his own. The smoke tasted good after the meal. A man should feel this way most of the time, he told himself.

He imagined the spread being his, the buildings, the cattle, the land, the woman inside. He imagined stepping outside the house after a fine full supper and having a cigarette and watching the sun sink red and feeling the coolness of evening start to come on.

She came outside, handed him a steaming mug of coffee and leaned against the wall next to him.

"What do you see, Mr. Dollar? Can you understand how a body could go crazy?"

"I reckon it must be hard on you, ma'am."

"Cows and cowboys," she said. "I don't see it. I was born in Ohio. There, we had trees and green grass and rivers . . . oh my, we had lots of water." She fell silent thinking about it. He crushed out his cigarette, not wanting to offend.

"I married Clave through the mail, answered his advertisement for a wife. I thought it would be a great adventure — you know, the wild and wooly West, marauding Indians, the frontier. My parents were against it of course, I was but seventeen at the time. I truly was a handsome girl, Mr. Dollar. I had many beaus at the time and could have taken my pick of men to marry."

Henry hitched his thumbs inside his pockets while he listened to her. She had a soft, mellow voice that belied her size.

"But I had a wild streak in me. Ohio was full of trees and grass and rivers and eager young farm boys, but it lacked adventure. It was a tamed land. When I saw Clave Miller's ad looking for a wife, I just naturally had to answer." She lapsed into silence again. He listened to her breathing.

"I reckon now I know."

"What's that?" he asked.

"Know that the whole thing was a mistake."

Silence, until the wind started up again, started up the blades of the windmill. *Clack. Clack. Clack. Clack.*

"Well, ma'am. It don't look like your man is likely to come back soon. I hate to take up more of your hospitality . . ."

"Stay."

Her long graceful fingers — too delicate for her big hands, it seemed — reached out and touched him on the arm.

"Ma'am?"

"Clave isn't coming back tonight. He and the hands have ridden to Mobeetie to visit the cathouse. They won't come riding in until tomorrow or the next day — else, they'd already be back by now. Clave don't miss supper unless he's gone to Mobeetie."

It seemed the gliding light of dusk had trans-

91

formed her, had softened her looks. She reached up and unpinned her hair and let it fall loose about her shoulders.

"I know I'm not pretty, not anymore I'm not. But it don't stop my desire to have a man treat me like I still am."

"I'm sure plenty of men would —"

"No, Mr. Dollar, that's not true. Why else would Clave ride all the way to Mobeetie to get what he can get here? I'm not a fool, Mr. Dollar. I'd take it as a kindness on your part if you'd spend the night with me." She allowed her hand to drop away and she turned her face back toward the open flatness of the land that had now grown to shadows.

He took her hand and held it for a time. And for a time, the two of them stood silent, each with their own thoughts.

He knew everything about it was wrong. Taking a man's horse or his woman was a killing offense. And if he did this thing, and Clave Miller showed up . . .

But she squeezed his hand, and he could hear the soft snuffling sound of her crying, and something in *that* touched him in a way that few other things in life ever had.

"I'd like to wash up, first," he said, just as the last ray of sun disappeared below the edge of the earth.

She leaned and kissed him gently on the cheek.

"There's a wash pan, soap, and towel out back. I'll be inside when you're finished."

"Are you sure this is something you want?" he asked.

"No, Mr. Dollar, I'm not sure at all. But, I know it is something I need."

Chapter Eight

It had been three days since he had ridden out of Ft. Smith. The crawly feeling up his back that someone was dogging his trail had not left him in all that time. Nights were getting downright spooky by his book.

He had found it hard to shut his eyes and sleep, even with a gut full of whiskey. He had grown to favor the whiskey too much — once a man craved *Old Tom* day and night, well, that told a feller something about himself — something that was hard to face each day he looked in the mirror.

He stayed to the trees, in amongst the tall pines, stayed clear of open ground whenever he could. Trouble was, a horse walked soft, hardly no sound at all on ground covered thick with pine needles. But a feller would have to shoot around an awful lot of trees to shoot him in the back, reasoned the old lawman.

He made dry camp the first two nights, but on the third day, it had rained and turned unusually cold — he rode in it for hours. By that night, he had gotten the shakes from being so cold and wet.

He found an old lean-to, all that was left of some old farm, it appeared. It wasn't much, but it had stopped raining and it seemed like wonderful shelter to spread out his war bag under.

He scrounged around the area and dug up some old lumber that had lain under a piece of tin roofing. It was dry enough to build a fire from.

He had hardtack and whiskey for a supper, but with the warmth of the fire at his feet, the hardtack and whiskey seemed just fine.

He gave only brief thought to the suspicion that someone was on his trail and that he was an easy target sitting there in the fire's light. *Well, to hell with it,* he told himself. *I'd just as soon be shot dead as to die of the pneumonia — what's the difference!*

He had his horse, a dapple gray mare, hobbled nearby and spoke to it openly. The whiskey was dulling his senses. The horse eyed him suspiciously whenever his voice grew loud.

"I was once a fire-eatin' son of a bitch!" he announced to the animal. "Now look at me, all broke down like a fat widow's sofa. Your back must be as sore as an infected tooth havin' to carry me around all day." His laugh was cut off by a hacking cough that he had come to notice more and more as of late.

"The damn croup's come to take me, Li'l Bess." He had named the mare after his late mother — in his mind, the greatest of all respects to be paid.

He coughed and swallowed more whiskey.

"I have shot men, and been shot!" he yelped, resuming his monologue to the encroaching night, to the grazing horse. "This saddle's had blood on it," he said, patting the worn leather

95

beneath his elbow. "*My* blood!"

"I've been cut with knives and been banged over the head. Had my jaw broke by a desperado named . . . named. . . ." He searched his fogged memory for the name of the man that had broken his jaw in a fight — what fight exactly, he could not recall either.

"Dick Treadwell! Mean son of a bitch! Prize-fighter! No wonder he broke my jaw." The fire was feeling warm and pleasant.

"Had a bad eye but could hit you with either hand quick as you could spit." He rubbed the jaw, remembering where Dick Treadwell had broken it, and grinned, showed old teeth in doing so.

The feeling came over him again, the feeling that someone was out there. He reached a hand out and touched the Winchester repeating rifle propped up against the trunk of a yellow pine. Then, partly for comfort, partly for assurance, he shifted the holstered .45 caliber single-action Colt off his hip and onto his lap, the worn walnut grips smooth to the touch. With seven and a half inches of barrel, it was a hefty piece.

"I don't know who the hell you are out there, mister! But if you've come to take my hide, you'll get hold of nothing but wild panther and poison!" The yelling made him short of breath, made him need another swallow of whiskey.

"I'll gouge out your eyeballs and eat them for breakfast!"

Sitting in the darkness, a silent form of a man

listened to the ranting of the drunken law-man.

Eli Stagg had planned on trailing the Deputy all the way to Ardmore, had planned on waiting until he took charge of the prisoners and then making his move.

After having used threat on the telegrapher back in Ft. Smith, threat that produced a look-see at the message being sent down to the Texas Rangers in Pecos, the bounty hunter figured it would just be a simple matter to hang on the trail of the careless old lawman.

But now, things had changed. The deputy had detected his presence — how, he wasn't sure. Never know, he thought, the old coot might set an ambush for him. Eli Stagg was not a man to take chances. *No, he'd have to kill the lawman. Kill him tonight.*

More whiskey, less fear. The drink had turned the old lawman maudlin. He remembered a song. His voice sang mournful.

"I asked my love to come with me. To take a walk a little way . . ." His voice broke with one great sob and then another. Tears slid down his cheeks, the words to the song momentarily lost within the clouded mind.

The old bastard was crying. Eli Stagg was forced to stifle a laugh. *Damn'd old fool.*

Al Freemont used his blue bandanna to blow his nose and clear his eyes. Another drink of old busthead and things would feel better, he told himself as he tilted the bottle to his lips.

The words of the song returned to him:

I held a knife against her breast, and gently in my arms she pressed. Crying: Willie, oh Willie, don't murder me. For I'm unprepared for eternity. . . .

It was a song that he had learned as a boy: *Banks of The Ohio.* Some of the words had become lost to time. It was the sad tale of a man who killed his lover and threw her body into the river because she refused to be his bride. It was exactly the sorry state of mind he wished to be in.

He closed his eyes, remembered a girl with carrot-colored hair, remembered the greenness of her eyes and the way she called him Albert. It seemed like such a long long time ago. He remembered a paint horse, and high-water pants, and a barn dance — remembered the sound of the fiddler's music and the smallness of her feet.

The snap of a twig somewhere close by cracked through the fog of his mind. He forced himself to lift his head off the saddle, leaned on one elbow and stared out at the blackness.

"Who's out there?" His right hand fumbled for the pistol. It had somehow gotten twisted underneath him: *Where was the damn thing!*

He sensed it rather than saw it — the presence of a man! The awareness startled him. The whiskey lay on him like a weight.

"Who — ?" His fingers touched the butt of the pistol — at last! But something pinned his wrist down, pressed it into the soft earth. Something soft. He realized it was a moccasined foot.

He reached with the other hand, but something struck him across the jaw and he fell back onto the saddle. He felt the pistol being jerked loose from his holster, saw the large shadow of a man loom over him silhouetted against the light of the campfire.

Then something cracked him hard in the ribs and he felt something snap within his chest, felt a great sharp pain that not even the whiskey would dull, felt his breath flee him for an instant.

He struggled to rise, struggled like he never had before. A sharp blow struck him just above the ear and he felt himself falling down what seemed a dark hole.

Eli Stagg brought the rifle stock of the Creedmore down for a second strike against the lawman's head, but it proved unnecessary; the man collapsed face down and did not move. There was a bloody gash just near the temple.

Eli Stagg breathed heavily as he stood over the lawman.

"I guess you've about sung the last you're ever goin' to," he said, checking the lawman for any sign of life. There was none.

The bounty hunter saw the near empty bottle of Foster's Blend Whiskey lying tipped over on its side. He reached for it, wiped dirt from the neck, and swallowed what was left.

"Well, at least you knew your likker," he said, tossing the empty bottle near the body.

He began a careful search of the lawman's pockets. There was little to be found: a plug of tobacco, a pocket knife, a stub pencil, some pennies and nickels.

Next, the bounty hunter searched the saddle-pockets lying on the ground near the bedroll; two more bottles of Foster's Blend, vouchers imprinted with a Federal stamp, obviously for the use of supplies, and some legal papers detailing the arrest warrant and transfer of the two prisoners — Johnny Montana and Katie Swensen.

One final thing. The bounty hunter unpinned the star from Al Freemont's coat. "I guess I'm the law now," he said with a grim satisfaction. "I guess maybe the law ain't so dern keen after all!"

Studying the script on the documents more closely, the killer saw that the deputy's name was Al Freemont. He was to make contact with the local law in Ardmore, the Indian Nations. The document would introduce him as being from Judge Parker's court of Federal Marshals. Further, the local law was ordered to assist in the transfer between a Texas Ranger by the name of Pete Winter and his prisoners in whatever way possible in order to expedite their return to the state of Arkansas to stand trial for murder.

It said some other things, too, legal parlance, which the bounty hunter neither understood or cared to understand. The main thing was, he had the documents and the badge, and soon, he'd have the two people that could bring him the rest of the reward money.

By now, he had even figured out how he was

going to show proof to that feller Kimbel. After he killed ol' Johnny Montana, he'd haul him to the nearest town and have his picture took. Damn if life wasn't gettin' simple.

Chapter Nine

The journey had been marked mostly by silence, except for the soft plodding of the horses' hooves.

Johnny Montana found lots to complain about: His handcuffs were chaffing his wrists, the ranger was being inconsiderate of the woman's delicacy in having to ride for such long stretches at a time, the thirst they had to endure, and of the all-round general poor treatment they were getting.

Pete Winter mostly ignored the outlaw's carping. His attention was given over to the woman, who rode in silence and without complaint. It was because of her that he allowed them to pause and rest more often along the trail than he otherwise would have.

They were nearing the end of their fifth day on the trail. Pete Winter decided they should make camp for the evening along a small tributary that was marked on his map as No Timber Creek.

As was his usual practice, the ranger draped a blanket over some small mesquite trees in order to provide a sheltered lean-to for the prisoners.

He removed the outlaw's wrist irons and allowed each of them to "take a little walk" of privacy. He knew that they wouldn't run; there was no place to go out on the open prairie, not without a horse there wasn't.

Afterwards, he placed leg irons on them and allowed them to sit in the shade of the lean-to while he prepared supper.

He built a fire from mesquite and set a pot of beans and a pan of bacon to cooking.

"How about some water, mister? My tongue's about fried out of my mouth!" Once more the outlaw was complaining.

Pete Winter took one of the canteens he had filled in the trickle of stream and walked it over to the couple. He handed it to the woman.

"Drink it down slow," he warned. "You swallow too much or too fast, it'll bring on cramps."

The outlaw reached out and snatched the canteen from her grasp. Pete Winter tore it from his hands before he could drink from it.

"You wait your turn, amigo!"

Johnny Montana's dark, sullen gaze came to bear on the lawman.

"I won't suffer your abuse just because you pack a gun and wear that little tin star on your shirt! You touch me again and I'll . . ."

Pete Winter's instinct was to jerk the man to his feet and knock some respect into him. But he remembered the Captain's admonishment about abuse to prisoners and so refrained. Instead, he steadied his youthful gaze upon the outlaw.

"Don't prod me, mister. My orders don't say how I have to deliver you to the authorities up in Ardmore. I can just as easily bring you in slung belly down across your saddle — it's not a good way to ride."

The threat seemed enough; the outlaw turned his stare away, looked out toward the open plains as though something else had suddenly drawn his interest.

Pete Winter returned to his cooking pots and stirred the beans and forked the bacon over. His thinking turned toward the woman. He felt sorry for her having been subjected to the outlaw's whims and most likely abuses.

The young lawman had seen much in his day, including women who suffered greatly under the hands of ruthless, insensitive men.

He thought of his own mother, of how before she died so early in life, she had come to bear the withered looks of a woman twice her age from the hard, unending work. He recalled how, even though he loved his father, the man had been joyless and single-minded in his determination to scratch out a life from dirt that didn't produce, and rain that didn't come, and dreams that never were.

The old man was good in that he never cussed his wife, never laid a hand upon her, but, he never showed her kindness either. He never saw how the life was killing her. And when she finally did pass away, the tears that slipped from his eyes were too little too late — just like the rain he always waited for had been too little too late.

The ranger understood how his mother's love for the old man had made her hold on longer than she should. And, even though he knew practically nothing at all about this woman who was now his prisoner, he knew that it had been *her* love for the outlaw that had brought her to this place. He understood that much about her.

His thoughts were interrupted by her voice.

"Maybe I could help with the cooking," she offered. It was the most she had said the whole trip. He turned and looked at her.

"It would be better than just sitting and doing nothing," she responded to his inquisitive gaze.

"Well, ma'am, we might all appreciate the grub better. I confess that cooking ain't the dang thing I do best."

"No reason for you to help out, Kate!" demanded Johnny Montana. "It'd be the same as you helping to get us back to Arkansas for our hanging."

"I'm weary of just sitting all day and all evening with nothing to do, Johnny! Helping out will take my mind off things." The ranger was both surprised and pleased by her rebuttal. He moved to where she sat and removed the leg irons.

"Be my guest," he said. "Anything you can do to make supper set better would get no argument from me." She smiled. So did he.

"Hell! I can see what this is all leading to," complained the outlaw. "Looks to me like he's in and I'm out as far as you're concerned, woman! I'd say you're being a damn'd fool — you're playing right into his hands, Katie!"

"You've got a bad mouth on you, mister, give it a rest!" ordered the lawman. "Ever since we started out, all you've done is complain and my ears have grown sore from your jawing. You leave off, or I'll gag you the rest of the trip!"

Johnny Montana fell sullen and silent, pouting like a disappointed child.

But, there was more than met the eye. The outlaw knew one thing for certain: the young ranger was unable to hide his interest in Katie. He knew full well how such a distraction could work for his favor. He knew just as well that a moment's worth of distraction was all it took to kill any man. He would bide his time, play the role of the jilted lover, let Katie, unwittingly, do her work. His time would come.

After supper, Johnny feigned tiredness and lay down upon his bedroll and closed his eyes, but not his ears.

"Well, ma'am, I have to tell you that adding a spoonful of sugar to those beans made all the difference," said the ranger.

"It would have been better if we would have had some molasses and onions," said Katie.

"It beat heck out of what I've done to the cooking the whole while," he said, apologetically.

"Don't know why men can't cook as well as women," she said. "I guess it's just because they're not taught to do so. I read that the best cooks in places like France and Spain are all men."

He stared at her across the flames of the fire, a curious look in his eyes.

"Oh, I once did a lot of reading, when I lived back home with papa. There wasn't much else to do. I so enjoyed reading about exotic places. I've always thought travel was adventuresome. To sail in a ship across the ocean — that would be so. . . ." Her voice trailed off. He could see her blinking her eyes, fighting back tears.

"I'm afraid that I will never know such things now." She failed to fight back all the tears. He could see the wet trace down her cheeks. He searched for something to say to her, to comfort her.

Seeing the way the soft light of the fire played upon her face caused him to stare.

She sniffled once, straightened her back and wiped her eyes with her fist.

"I'm sorry," she said. "I did not mean to seem like such a ninny. I've done what I've done, and now I must face up to it. My only wish would be to see my papa again and tell him how sorry I am for the grief and pain I have caused him. If I have hurt anyone, it was him."

"Perhaps things won't turn out as bad as they seem," said Pete Winter.

"You are kind for trying to buck up my spirits, Mr. Winter. But, I expect the worst to come of it. I must prepare myself for that end."

He was a handsome boy, she thought. Even though they were most likely the same age, she felt much older than him. She saw Johnny, lying there sleeping as though he had not a care in the world. And even though Johnny was not much older, he seemed a man far advanced in years. He seemed an outlaw.

"It seems all so strange," she said, as though speaking aloud to herself rather than directly to the lawman. "Not all that long ago, I thought that

Johnny Montana was my Prince and I the maiden he had come to rescue. He seemed so handsome and daring. It was his wild daring that I fell for . . ."

He felt he could not take his eyes off her.

"There was a time, Mr. Winter, when I would have done nearly anything for him . . . I suppose I did. Except for murder. But, in truth, Mr. Winter, I am no better than he."

"I guess we all make mistakes." He worked a mesquite limb into the coals of the fire. "I reckon we've all done things we're not proud of."

His words helped it seemed, or maybe it was just the fact that she had someone to really talk to after all these months. She sensed her father's kindness in him and wondered why all men were not possessed of such kindness. Why could Johnny Montana not have been instilled with such kindness?

"Look at the stars, Mr. Winter. The night is full of stars. They seem to me as exotic and mysterious as France or Spain. Do you think that after we die that we live among the stars?"

"I don't reckon I'd know, Miss Swensen. It's something I confess that I have not given any attention to."

"Of course not," she said, a smile greeting his glance as he lowered his eyes from the star-filled night.

"When we're young, death should not be part of our thoughts. But imagine what it would be like to have wings and fly up there. . . ."

"It surely would be something," he said, returning his attention heavenward. He thought of how, exactly, it would feel to be able to fly. He thought of what it would be like to come to know the woman across the fire from him now. She had a way of talking, a way of thinking about things that he had had little experience at. It was something that interested him. She interested him.

"Look, there's a shooting star," she said, pointing like an excited child might.

He saw the streak of light, the meteor's trail, and it captured his imagination. He felt a pang of sorrow in that brief instant, a sorrow that spoke of a long ago childhood, of a loving mother whose life had been just as brief and fleeting as the comet's had been, of a father who had afterwards delivered him up to the doorstep of Captain Ben Goodlow and said only: "He's a good boy but I don't have it in me to raise him now that his ma has passed," and then had ridden away.

It seemed as though the woman's sorrow had become his own. But, just as he was unable to rid himself of his own pain, he knew of no good way to help her get rid of hers.

"My papa used to tell me that if you saw a shooting star and made a wish before it disappeared, your wish would come true," she said.

"Did you make a wish?" he asked.

"No," she said.

"Why not?"

"I guess because I don't believe that it would happen. I believe that my papa was only a man who loved to tell his little girl stories that would make her happy. I'm no longer a little girl, Mr. Winter. And, I am no longer happy."

Chapter Ten

It wasn't until the next morning, when he awoke, lying in the small sleigh bed, his head on a turkey feather pillow, awoke to the sound of her singing down the hallway, that he realized that he never asked her her name.

He had wanted to call out to her, to tell her to come back to the bedroom and sit on the side of the bed so he could look at her, so he could touch her hand once more, or stroke her hair, which had been soft and fragrant and womanly. It was then that he realized that he did not know her name.

He realized too that he was sleeping in another man's bed, and that the woman singing in the other room was another man's wife. Whatever thoughts he was having of her were thoughts he had no right thinking.

But still, he lingered for a moment more before rising and dressing.

"Good morning, Mr. Dollar," she said brightly as he entered the kitchen; the smell of coffee and frying ham, along with the sound of her singing, had drawn him to find her there.

"Ma'am," he said, now embarrassed that he could not call her by name.

"Seems like we ought to be past, ma'am," she said. "My name is Josepeth, but I'd be offended if you called me that. Josie is what I prefer."

"Josie," he said, settling on a high back chair at the table, the one he had sat on the evening before to eat the supper she had provided him.

She poured him a mug of coffee and came and set it before him before drawing a chair close and sitting by him. She smelled fresh, smelled of soap and rosewater. Her hair was still down; she wore a cotton night dress that had lace at the neck and at the wrists.

"Do you find me shameless, Mr. Dollar?"

"No, ma . . . no, Josie, I don't find you so in any way."

She leaned forward and kissed him lightly. He had not shaved, his face was rough with an old growth of whiskers. She had not complained.

"Would you go for a ride with me after breakfast?" she asked.

"Mr. Miller?" he asked.

"Probably won't come home until toward evening," she said. He could see disappointment cross her face at the mention of her husband.

"His usual pattern when he rides to Mobeetie is to spend the night, and ride back the next day, but, as you know, it is a full day's ride. And that's if he doesn't decide to stay a second night in Mobeetie. He usually doesn't." She leaned and kissed him again. He didn't mind how it felt. He reached and touched her hair, felt its long smoothness against the palm of his hand.

"Besides, Mr. Dollar, you do have business to discuss with him, so it would not be all that unusual if you were waiting for him when he arrived."

"I must admit, Josie, that the idea of spending the day with you is appealing. I find myself favoring you and being here more than I have a right to."

"Mr. Dollar, I will not put up a fuss if you feel it goes against your grain to stay the day. I believe you a man of good moral character, did from the minute you rode up yesterday, or I would not have offered that you stay. In spite of what has taken place, I do not consider myself a loose woman. But, you have to know, I am feeling as beautiful and desirable as any woman could possibly feel, and I'd like to hold onto that feeling as long as I can."

Whether it was her plain wholesome looks, or her way of speaking matter-of-factly with him about her feelings, everything about her agreed with him.

"Josie," he began. "I don't know what your man is like, but he must be the biggest fool in the Panhandle to spend his time anywhere else other than here."

Her eyes teared, she blinked quickly.

"Did I say the wrong thing?"

"No, Mr. Dollar. You said exactly the right thing."

After breakfast he saddled the buckskin and a chestnut mare she said was hers and they rode for several miles to where the tributaries of the Canadian and the Rita Blanca forked. She had brought along a picnic lunch and they allowed the horses to graze on the tall grass along the banks while they spread a black and red checked blanket on the ground.

They sat for a time listening to the waters spilling their way south and west, spilling their way to some unknown destination.

The wind blew gentle for once. The sky was blue and cloudless overhead; the air, warm and pleasant.

"It's my favorite place," she said, leaning her head on his shoulder. "When I first came here eighteen years ago, the Comanches watered their horses at this very spot. You could not come here alone — they were very fierce toward the white man then. We would come in groups, wagons full of us, to picnic. The men would all keep their guns handy, though. But we were never disturbed by the Comanches or any other Indians. This place seems less special without them," she sighed.

"Well, there's still a few bands roaming around yet," he said. "Renegades, not the same type as you would have known back then. The ones raiding and running around now — those still wild — they're not the same. They don't have pride in who they are, or were. They're just mostly outlaws and aren't to be trusted."

"We've taken all the adventure out of it, haven't we, Mr. Dollar?"

"Ma'am?"

"We've tamed the Indians, tamed the land, and someday we'll probably figure out a way to tame the weather. It does not seem like much of a place to be anymore."

"No, Josie, it doesn't. And, in some ways I miss it and what it was, even though what it was wasn't always pleasant. I guess the only thing we haven't tamed are the white men. We still got a passel of them that can sure stir things up. I guess, in a way, I ought not to be too disappointed: it gives me work and wages. But, the older I get, the less I feel up to it.

"It wouldn't be so bad, having a little spread like you and Mr. Miller have got, a nice little herd of longhorns, and. . . ."

"And what, Mr. Dollar?"

"And a woman like you."

She pressed her head against him, her arm around his waist.

"Why should it be," she said, "that I'd have to meet you now instead of eighteen years ago?"

"Maybe eighteen years ago, we wouldn't have recognized the value in one another," he said.

"Oh, I would have recognized it in you, Mr. Dollar. A man such as yourself would be hard not to notice, then or now."

"Well maybe," he said. "But, back then, I wasn't quite the same person as I am today."

"What were you back then, Mr. Dollar? How were you so different than you are now?"

"Well, for one thing, I was as wild as a wooly range bronc," he laughed, and in so doing realized how long it had been since he had laughed aloud. It felt good.

"Up until the war came along to give me a whole new perspective on things, I thought the world was just there for my enjoyment."

"And what did you do for enjoyment?" she teased.

"Well, Josie, I'm not so sure an Ohio girl should hear such things." He gave her a wink that she found charming.

"Mr. Dollar, I have not been an Ohio girl for some time and I know all about such places as they have in Mobeetie and why men go there."

"I must confess, that I have myself spent a time or two in such places as you describe are in Mobeetie. And, I have tasted whiskey and admit to liking it on occasion, but now favor tequila somewhat better. And, I have gotten falling down drunk a time or two."

Her laughter triggered his own and they rolled on the blanket until there were tears in their eyes.

And when they finally caught their breath, they lay for a long time holding hands and looking into one another's eyes.

"Do you remember yesterday when you asked me if I thought you were pretty?" he asked after a time.

"Yes."

"I told you that I thought most man would find your looks agreeable."

"Yes, I recall you telling me that."

"Well, Josie. I lied. At the time I was just trying to tell you what I thought you wanted to hear." He saw the change in her face, saw the flash of disappointment.

"What I should have said, and what I *am* saying

116

to you is, I find you one of the most lovely women I have ever known. The more I look, the more I see."

This time, she could not stop the tears from coming, nor did she want to.

"You make me very happy, Mr. Dollar."

"I reckon the easiest thing for me to do would be to say the same thing, Josie." And then it was his turn to kiss her.

"Have you ever had the fortune to make love to a woman on the prairie, Mr. Dollar?"

"No, ma'am, I have not."

"Well, your fortune is about to change."

Afterwards, they ate fried chicken, powdered biscuits and honey, canned peaches, boiled potatoes, pickled eggs, and drank buttermilk from a jar that they had kept cold by submerging in the flowing waters of the Canadian. She had also included two large slices of apple pie, which they took turns feeding one another.

Somewhere the hours had flown.

"I should be getting you back, Josie, before Mr. Miller arrives," he said reluctantly.

"We could just keep riding," she said, her hazel eyes serious. "We could just ride off in any direction we wanted to and find a life for ourselves."

"It'd be mighty easy for me to say yes. But, I guess if we did it that way, I wouldn't ever be able to feel right about it, and, I don't think you would either. Not in the long run."

They both knew that he was right.

They rode back to the ranch at a slow, reluctant pace, each silent in their thoughts, each wanting to say something to the other that would offer hope.

She had just finished putting away the picnic supplies while Henry leaned against the house smoking a cigarette when three riders appeared on the east road.

"That will be Mr. Miller," she said coming outside to stand next to the ranger. The hour had grown late, the sky had turned brassy.

"The two men with him are occasional hands that share their time between spreads around here. Tip Wymans and Ollie Hunt."

The trio reined in.

"Who might you be, mister? And what are you doing here alone with my wife?"

Clave Miller was a common looking man, the only physical exception being that his ears stuck out like the doors of a barn left open.

"I'm a Texas Ranger," replied Henry, crushing the cigarette under the heel of his boot. He lifted back the flap of his duster enough for Clave Miller and the two that rode with him to see the badge he wore.

"Josie, you know how I feel about strangers hanging around here — you know what I've warned you about."

Maybe because of his feelings toward the woman, his opinion of the man was colored, but he instantly did not care for Clave Miller.

"Like I said, Mr. Miller, I'm a Texas Ranger.

118

Your missus is not the reason I'm here. I came on official business." The explanation did not seem to appease the man, however. He continued to glare at his wife.

"You care to inform as to exactly *why* it is that you have come here, ranger?"

"Was reported that cattle were being rustled, enough so as to have a formal request made to investigate," said Henry, doing his best to maintain some official decorum with the man.

"Well sir, cattle rustling is about as old a profession as there is around here. That, and whorin'. Ain't that right boys?" It seemed to Henry that the man enjoyed being crude in front of his wife.

The two men at his side grinned their approval.

"Then I take it, Mr. Miller, that you have not suffered any stealing from your herds?"

"Hell yes I've had stock stolen. But, so what? So has everybody else in the Panhandle. What you don't understand is that we take care of our own problems up here. We don't need the Texas Rangers, or anyone else for that matter. Now if you don't mind, get the hell off my property or else I will be forced to have you shot!"

The lawman stiffened at the challenge. All three riders were wearing sidearms, and all three had Winchester stocks showing from saddleboots. Whether they were true gunhands or not, he could only guess.

"Why are you being so mean-minded, Clave?" Josie, full of scorn, stepped between them, and said, "You've been drinking!"

"You keep your mouth shut, woman! Stay clear of men's business!" Her entry into the fray had only provoked the rancher. Henry Dollar had been a lawman for a long time and he knew when small matters got out of hand, they could turn dangerous, more dangerous than they ought to be.

Gunplay wasn't called for here. He didn't think the cowboys were gunfighters and Clave Miller looked more bark than bite. But still, there was Josie to consider.

"There's no need, ma'am," he said, meeting her gaze. "I'll be on my way." He could see the look of disappointment and doubt in her eyes.

He turned his attention to the rancher.

"I'll be around these parts for a few days," he said more as a warning than as plain conversation.

"Ain't no concern of mine, mister. You just watch whose property you're tramping on." The double meaning didn't escape the lawman's notice.

"Don't push your luck compadre!"

He turned to go, paused and said, "Ma'am, if I might have a word with you in private for a moment." Clave Miller started to speak, but the lawman's glance warned him off.

He walked her out of earshot.

"Josie, I'll be back around this way. I haven't figured everything out yet — about you and me. I haven't figured out how it is we should say our goodbyes to one another."

She glanced once over her shoulder, saw that her husband was watching them, straining, as if to hear the conversation.

"I'm not ready to say goodbye to you, Henry. I'm just not."

"I guess I'm not so ready, either."

"I could go with you now. I'd be willing."

"A few days," he said. "Let us both think about it for a few days."

"A few days then, Mr. Dollar."

"Yes, Josie. A few days."

She watched him ride away, and her heart rode with him. And even after he had disappeared she could still feel his presence.

Chapter Eleven

They had ridden into the blackness of the night. The dank smells of the swamp filled their nostrils. Something with great flapping wings flew across the road before them. A chorus of night creatures rose and fell from the brackish waters.

They had ridden for the better part of an hour since having fled the house in New Orleans. A full moon was just beginning its ascent above the tangled tops of cypress trees.

Lowell Biggs rode slumped over the horn of his saddle; each jolting step of the animal brought him greater pain. He struggled for every breath. The place in his back where the knife had gone in burned and squeezed at his lungs. He could feel the last of his strength draining away. Twice, he had nearly tumbled from his horse, but was held in the saddle by his brother.

But now, the last of him was bleeding out, and the pain had grown so terrible that he no longer cared if he went on. If he could only lay down and close his eyes and sleep for a little while, he told himself, everything would be fine.

Something blinked yellow in among the trees. The light of a cabin.

Carter saw it, pulled up alongside his brother and put his hand on the wounded man to steady him. "There," he said, pointing toward the small frame of light. "We'll get you some relief there!"

Lowell was too weak to reply. His body ran hot and cold with chills and fever.

As they approached the cabin, a dog came off the porch, its hackles raised, its snapping bark echoing into the night.

"Shut up!" yelled Carter at the hound as it stood its ground in front of the cabin. Carter reached for his pistol and was about to draw it and shoot the dog when the door of the cabin sprung open.

"Who be out there!" The voice was that of a woman; the accent, Cajun.

"Call off your hound, woman, or I'll shoot him!" demanded Carter. "I've got a wounded man that needs help!"

The dog's bark intensified at the sound of the stranger's voice. Carter lifted the pistol out of his holster and aimed it at the cur. The click of the hammer being thumbed back seemed insignificant but the barking gave way to a sudden low growl. The dog clearly recognized the sound of a revolver being cocked.

The woman said something in French or Cajun, Carter couldn't be sure which, something short and hard, something commanding. The dog eased back to her, came to stand by her feet switching its attention between her and the strangers.

Carter holstered the weapon, dismounted and eased Lowell from his saddle. Lowell whimpered in pain. Carter felt the coldness of his flesh.

Without bothering to ask permission, Carter half carried Lowell toward the cabin, up the few steps of the porch, past the woman, and brought the wounded man to rest upon a small cot in the corner of the single room.

"What is this you do here, eh?" she asked, falling in behind them. Reflected in the yellow light coming from an oil lamp on a table in the center of the room, the woman saw the bloody trail on the floor.

Carter turned his attention to her. She looked to be of color, but not exactly Negro. He had heard tell of the Cajun people in this part of the country, knew that many were of a mixed blood. He guessed her to be one.

She was a decent looking woman, he thought, eyes black as pitch, hair the same color — long, touching past her shoulders — skin the color of creamy coffee. She wore a simple cotton dress, no shoes.

"My brother's been stabbed in the back. He's nearly bled to death. I can't help it your's is the first place we come to. But he can't go no farther. I'll need clean water and rags to pack the wound, and what ever else you got to stanch the blood."

He saw her staring at him, staring at Lowell and where the blood was already soaking into the blanket that covered the cot.

"I'll pay for the convenience," he said.

"He is young," she said.

"Too damn young to die like this," said Carter, his impatience growing. "I could use that water and clean rags now!"

Without further comment, the woman went to a pitcher and poured water into a tin basin. She brought it to him and then opened a small trunk and removed a man's white shirt. She tore it into strips and gave them to him as well.

She stood aside and watched as the man cut the clothing from his brother's back with a small jack-knife he produced from his pocket. After swabbing the wound with a dampened rag, she could see the place where the man had been stabbed high on the back.

The wound glistened bloody in the light, the flesh around it dark purple. Small clots of bloody tissue oozed from it. The water in the pan swirled pink.

"I'll need to cauterize it," Carter said, his face knotted in sweat. "Do you have a flat piece of iron around here?"

She nodded toward a poker standing near a small open fireplace whose fire was little more than glowing embers, remnants from an earlier fire. "It'll have to do," he said.

He rekindled the fire and laid the blunt end of the poker on the burning chunks of wood until the metal glowed orange.

Lowell had lost consciousness, and Carter was glad that he had done so. "Hold his arms, sister," he ordered the woman. "Even though he's out, soon as I lay this iron on him, he'll come out screaming!"

The cabin filled with the smell of burning flesh and the horrible screams of a man being burnt. The pain had brought him to, and then sent him back to that deep dark place of unconsciousness.

125

Afterwards, Carter dressed the wound with a clean pack of white cloth and covered him with the blanket — the part that was not already bloody.

The whole time the woman had stood watching him in measured silence.

Carter stood, paced the room for a time, and then settled his gaze, first upon his brother's shallow breathing, and then upon the woman.

"He's going to die, I can feel it," he said.

The woman crossed in front of him, went to the bed and stood beside it, looking down on the wounded man.

"Maybe I can save him, eh?" she said.

"Don't know how, sister. The blade's broken off inside him. He's been bleeding for an hour or better already. Don't see how."

"I will need to be alone with him," she said. "To invoke the Spirits. They will not come if an outsider is here with us."

"Oh no, sis. He's in the shape he's in because I left him alone once already with a woman. I'm not leaving him alone with anybody!"

"Then he will die, as you have predicted," she said simply and turned away from the bed.

She looked strange, talked strange, and acted strange. He did not trust her. But still, Lowell was a goner as far as he could determine. He recalled hearing how people down in this country had strange ways, strange beliefs. Maybe she had some potion or some strange medicine that these people used to cure themselves. She surely must know something to do if she offered in the first

126

place. Lowell was dying, and quickly it looked like.

"Alright! Alright! You do what you know how to do to help him. It works, I'll be owing you." A burst of unexpected emotion caused him to consent to the strange, spooky woman.

"Okay."

He waited outside. The air was warm and humid. The dog eyed him suspiciously, growled once, and skulked away into the darkness.

He sat on the edge of the porch and made himself a cigarette and smoked it. He could hear the croak of what seemed a thousand frogs off in the night. Back and forth they called across the black soupy waters of the unseen swamp. There came a heavy splash in the water and the frogs all fell to silence for a few moments and then slowly began again, like a creaky wheel starting up.

A second sound began to come from within the cabin itself. A sound like no other he had heard before. A low moaning sound that rose steadily in pitch. It was the woman's voice, but not a voice so much as a wailing, a mourning cry. The sound made his skin crawl.

The sound brought him to his feet. He crossed the porch and peered in the window. Lowell's bed was completely surrounded by lighted candles, the many tongues of flames casting his sallow features in ghostly stillness — a halo of peacefulness.

My God, he has died, thought Carter.

The woman held something in her hand, something that appeared to be the talon of an owl. It was attached to a gourd rattle. She shook it vigorously over the supine form of the wounded man and chanted something unintelligible.

Her head was cast back, her eyes closed, her body trembling as she stood over the bed. The perspiration on her dark skin glistened in the candles' glow. Her upper body began to sway back and forth, her head tossed the raven black hair into flying streamers. She sang and sang, but in a language he could not hope to understand.

He felt a strangeness come over him as he watched her through the window, felt himself being roused by the gyrating brown body, by the unnatural sounds coming from her throat. He was mesmerized by the flicker of candle flames, by the peaceful stillness of Lowell's youthful face.

With great effort, he pushed himself away from the window and toward the edge of the porch, drank in the night air and steadied himself. He made another cigarette and smoked it.

"God damn your soul, Johnny Montana," he said to the darkness. "Damn your soul for bringing my family all this misery!"

He rested his back against the wall of the cabin and felt the heavy weight of the day descend upon him. The woman's voice had ceased to wail, but still, he could hear her inside, mumbling something, something in a low soothing voice.

He was bone-tired. He closed his eyes and saw the events of the day there in the dark warmth of his skull.

He awakened to the trilling of birds, to the warmth of sun upon his face. He had fallen asleep there on the porch of the cabin. His eyes cracked open. He saw a pair of brown feet, then the hem of the woman's skirt.

He sat up. She had been standing there watching him; for how long, he could only guess. He shook off the mantle of sleep, rubbed it from his eyes, worked it from his joints by stretching.

"How's Lowell?" he asked, dreading the answer he would receive.

"He is breathing easier," she said. "But, all danger has not left him yet. I have done all that is possible to do. I have called upon the Spirits. I have invoked the Power. But, his wound is mighty bad."

"I'll have a look-see for myself, sister." He entered the small cabin and went to the cot where Lowell lay belly down, his arms dangling off the sides. His breathing was steady but shallow, and once he moaned. For Carter, it seemed a pitiful sight.

He turned his attention to the woman who stood in the doorway.

"He's in poor shape," he said, looking at her as if for confirmation. When none was forthcoming, he said, "This could take some time — him getting better, or . . . passing on." Still, the woman made no comment.

"I'm sorry this all had to fall upon your head," he told her. "But, like I explained last night, there wasn't any other choice."

She moved to the small wood stove where she had been brewing a pot of coffee. The smell was strange.

"Chicory," she said.

"Look sister," he said. "I have to ride out after a man I'm looking for. The longer I wait, the less chance there is to find this feller. There's already been a long enough delay as it is."

She offered him sugar for his coffee. He held off.

"I'm willing to strike a bargain with you, sis," he said, looking around the small spare cabin.

"I'm willing to pay you good money, if you'll keep Lowell here until he can heal up. It sure looks like you could use some good money."

"I'm not a physician," she said. "I am only poor Marie, who lives in the bayou, eh. Does what she can, catch the fish, cook crawdads, eh. What you want from Marie anyway?"

"Like I said," he continued. "All I want is for you to see to him, change his bandages, take care of him, until he gets better."

"What if he die, then what?"

"Then . . . get somebody to help you bury him. Pay them if you have to, I'll leave you enough money."

"I don't know."

For the first time, she took the time to study this man who sat across from her and demanded so much. He was not a bayou man, that was easy enough to see from his color. Bayou men were dark, like the swamps — lean, and hard like cy-

130

press roots. This man was big and pink-skinned and had hair the color of old straw. This man did not speak like a Cajun, but his tongue was thick with accent.

Mostly what she noticed about the man who sat sipping the chicory coffee was that there was no smile to him, no fire down in his belly.

Her reluctance was beginning to fray his nerves. He was not accustomed to bargaining with women. Still, she held all the cards, he knew that much. If she refused to care for Lowell, he had little choice but to put him on a horse and find some sort of sanctuary — but where?

"I could shoot you for refusing to help," he said, but without conviction.

"You can kill Marie, that's for sure. But, I'm not afraid of you."

She saw the helplessness in his expression, the dogged creases around the eyes, the unsteady mouth.

"Well, sister, if you won't take my money and you won't take my threats, then I guess I just gather up my little brother and we'll be on our way." He pulled a wad of paper money from his pocket, peeled off some of it and placed it on the table near her coffee cup.

"That's for what you've done so far, for the night's stay, and the bandages and the coffee." He said, standing to his full height.

"I will take care of him," she said. "That fellow, he cannot go out. Such a thing would kill him."

Carter blew a sigh of relief. And for once in

131

his life, he felt grateful for another's help.

"Thanks sis."

"You sit and have some cooking before you go first, eh?"

He was anxious to get started, but a warm meal seemed too much to refuse.

He finished the last of it, noting the bite of its flavor.

Swiping at his plate with a piece of hard brown bread, he cleaned the last of the meal.

"You are lucky you did not come to old man Thibideux's place up the road there," she said, pointing with her nose. "He would have shot you, *Bang, Bang, Bang,* and then asked you what you want." Her laughter filled the room.

"I guess we could not have afforded anymore bad luck than what we've had lately," he said. She was surprised to see him smile, even though it was a faint one.

"Mr. Thibideux sounds like the kind of fellers we got back home in Autuaga County."

"Where is that place you say, eh?"

"Oh, it's a ways from here. A place called Alabama." He found himself enjoying her company, her conversation, her questions. "It's where me and Lowell lives."

"What you do in that place?"

"You mean what kind of work do we do?" She nodded. "Well, we have us a hog farm, more than two hundred head on about one-hundred and sixty acres. It ain't bottom land though, but it's good enough for raising hogs on."

132

Half of what he said was foreign to her, but she enjoyed the way he spoke of this Alabama.

"How you have so much land, eh?"

He scratched the stubble of beard growth on his cheek and realized that it had been some time since he had attended to his daily toilet. The sourness of his clothes was also apparent.

"Who this fella you after, eh?"

He pushed his plate away. His pile of crawdad shells was twice that on the woman's plate and he realized how hungry he had been.

"The feller's name is Johnny Montana. He murdered our pap. Killed him over a handful of cards."

"So, you chase after this fella what killed your pa-pa," she said, her eyes wet with curiosiry. "And when you catch him, then you take your revenge, eh?"

"That's about the size of it, sister."

"You call me Marie, eh?"

"Sure, sure."

"What if this man he kill you first?"

"Well, it ain't going to happen that way, Marie. I'm going to catch him and kill him, and that's going to be the end of it."

Her question had added to his own doubt about the mission he had set for both him and his brother.

Ever since the gunfight of the night before, he had turned the whole thing over in his head. A part of him was willing to give it up, to turn back. As much as it seemed unlikely, he found himself missing home and even the dern hogs.

133

The guilt of such thoughts nagged at him like a bad tooth.

For several long minutes he sat there in silence. Finally, the woman spoke.

"Well, you had better not be wasting so much more time in this place if you are going to catch that fella and kill him, eh?"

"I reckon so." He stood and walked to the bed where Lowell lay curled up in a peaceful sleep.

Turning to the woman, he said, "I'll leave his horse. You know anything about caring for horses, Marie?"

"Of course," she said. "Marie know about all creatures, not just people, eh."

"That ol' mare's pretty content just to graze, but a bag of oats now and again might not hurt her."

The woman nodded.

"Well, that'll 'bout do it then. I get back this way soon's I can. You tell Lowell what I've done, once he comes around."

She watched him from the porch until he was gone.

Chapter Twelve

They had continued to ride in a Northeasterly trek and were now nearing the southernmost portion of the Llano Estacado — the Staked Plains.

Treeless and void of all life it seemed, except for the vast fields of yuccas, their tall bone-white stalks shifting in the wind, the Staked Plains seemed a desperate stretch of land.

Pete Winter had crossed this land once before, and remembered it as merciless. There was some water, but it was hard to find. There were a few spreads, but few and far between.

It was known mostly for two things: badmen and renegade bands of Comanches. Because of its hostile nature, only the evil intentioned found it to be a place worth habituating.

The Comanches had once roamed this land with impunity. Great horsemen, and proud, they were a force to be reckoned with by any invader. But a fierce and pitched battle at Adobe Walls, in which they suffered immeasurable losses, announced their end as commanders of the Plains.

Afoot, they were awkward and slow. Astride their ponies, however, there was not a more graceful or deadly an enemy.

Pete Winter had never encountered these people, but he took it on good account as to their prowess. And it was of no little concern to him that there were still a few marauding bands of these warriors around.

Now, the trio paused and rested for a matter of minutes. He had them air their horses by loosening the saddles. While Johnny Montana and Katie Swensen took their ease, Pete Winter checked the supply of ammunition that he maintained in his saddlebags.

His weaponry consisted of a .44 caliber rimfire Winchester that held sixteen rounds, and .45 Colt single-action revolver. He had also packed a .45 Smith and Wesson Schofield break-top model. He hoped it was enough to get the job done.

The land ahead seemed without life. No movement, not even the scuttle of a lizard. Something in it made him feel uneasy.

He removed one of the canteens and held it out to the woman. As he did so, he gave a shifting glance toward the outlaw who made no attempt to reach for it first.

He watched her drink, and then hand it to Johnny Montana. "Go easy, mister," he cautioned the outlaw. "We've got a dry stretch ahead of us according to this map and my memory. This land won't forgive us if we run dry."

The outlaw cast a furtive glance at the lawman, but limited his take of the warm water. Pete Winter drank last, taking in the least amount he thought necessary. They still had two full canteens, but there was no telling when the next water might appear. Many of the marked sources on the map the ranger carried had proved to be either dried up, or not where they were marked.

When he finished drinking, he hooked the canteen over the horn of his saddle, and grabbed the pair of handcuffs and tossed them to the outlaw.

"This land looks like hell and brimstone, ranger. A man could easily lose himself and die out here. We ain't lost are we?"

"Mount your horse, mister," was the only response Pete Winter cared to give.

He did not feel lost, but finding good water was beginning to concern him. For the last several hours, he had scanned the ground looking for animal tracks that might lead to water. He had seen none.

He moved to help the woman mount up. In order to do so, he had to form a stirrup with his hands while she gripped the horn and cantel and pulled herself up. She weighed practically nothing at all, it seemed to him.

For Katie Swensen, the trip had confirmed one glaring fact for her: Each mile crossed caused her to become more bitter and sorry for her decision to have run away with Johnny Montana.

Each time she glanced at him, she no longer saw the gallant, handsome man who had entered her father's store that fateful day. Rather, she saw an embittered, complaining, weak soul whose only concern seemed to be his own discomfort. She had asked herself a hundred times or more since their capture why she had ever been so foolish.

She felt the heavy weight of guilt riding with her. *Yes*, she told herself, she was just as guilty as he for the crimes that were committed. He had done those things, but she had stayed with him. It seemed of little consolation to her that she could tell herself she had acted out of love for the man.

Now, as she stole glances at him, all she saw was a man whose wrists were shackled, a man who exuded sweat and meanness and arrogance. She saw now, not a handsome sweetheart, but a dejected, captured outlaw.

Her heart was full of gloom.

The small renegade band of Comanches came across the fresh tracks of horses.

One of the warriors dropped from his pony and read the sign, the tips of his brown fingers tracing the hoofed depressions.

Three sets of tracks indicated they were shod horses; the fourth set appeared to be that of the Long-Ear animal the white man used to pack supplies. The warrior made sign by holding up three fingers and then using his fingers to make ears atop his head to indicate the riders were packing supplies on a mule.

He pointed off toward the direction that the tracks were leading. The Comanches knew the land well. They knew it to be a dry, harsh environment that could parch a man's throat and swell his tongue black in the summer, freeze him to death in the winter.

The band had been returning from a raiding party in the New Mexican Territory. The raid had netted them little save one milch cow, which they had ended up slaughtering for food. Now, they had a quarry at hand . . . only three riders.

Their leader, an extremely muscular man, looked off toward the direction the tracker had pointed. Waves of heat rose off the floor of the land and blurred his vision beyond a point.

They too were in search of water. There was good water less than an hour's ride, but in the opposite direction that the tracks of the shod horses were headed. Their skin water bag was nearly empty.

The leader of the group considered the options: *The chase would lead them away from water. He knew of no good water in the direction the tracks were leading. If the riders who had left the tracks were well-armed, it could come down to a fight where braves would be lost. He knew some of the whites to be good shooters and repeating rifles could make few seem like many.*

The tracker made a short grunt followed by a hand signal that expressed his impatience at not pursuing the horse tracks.

The leader made a gesture to cut off the tracker's impudence. He weighed, for a moment more, the decision. The lack of water for themselves and their ponies could prove a difficult problem if they did not catch up to the quarry quickly. On the other hand, the prospect of catching more horses and possibly prisoners was an attractive motivation.

The dark eyes within the coppery face searched the direction the riders had ridden off. His pony, too, seemed to be impatient as it stamped and pawed at the ground.

Finally, with a broad grin splitting his round face, he signalled them forward in the direction of the tracks. They yipped their approval.

To count coup, to take scalps, to steal the enemy's horses, that was the way of the true Comanche.

The shadows of the three riders and their animals grew long over the plains. The fiery sun had made its trek from east to west across a cloudless sky.

For the better part of the last hour, Pete Winter and his prisoners had been following a dry wash that snaked across the flat ground. Even though dry, the fact that it existed at all gave the ranger some hope that it might eventually lead to water.

Earlier, they had spotted a jackrabbit hunched beneath a greasewood bush. It had broken cover as they neared and quickly disappeared among the many yucca. It was a missed opportunity for some meat, but, the ranger concluded, it might mean that water was near.

They rode on.

The small band of Comanche warriors were closing fast on their quarry; the tracks were growing fresher. They rode proud, haughtily upon their ponies. Some possessed Henry model 1866 repeating rifles, their stocks studded with brass tacks. The others carried old breech-loading, single-shot Springfield carbines. They wore no paint, except the paint of dust that clung to their coppery skins.

When they would find water, they would cover themselves with mud to stave off the heat and sting of insects.

They carried war shields of painted hide. And one or two carried the old weapons of bows and rabbit fur quivers full of arrows.

"I've got to stop for a time, ranger!" announced Montana. "It's that time of day for me. You got any more of those catalogue pages left from that book?"

Pete halted the group and allowed the outlaw to dismount and walk off toward a distant yucca plant. The ranger dismounted and helped Katie Swensen to do the same. She had a pale, haggard appearance.

He sat her down on the ground and handed her a canteen. Taking the bandanna from around his neck, he handed that to her as well.

"Wet it down and tie it around your neck," he offered. "It'll help cool you down."

She smiled wanly, her eyes pretty but sad.

"Thank you, mister," she said, spilling enough water on the bandanna to wet it down and then pressing it to her face.

"No need for thanks," he said. "And you can call me, Pete. Mister sounds sort of old."

She lifted her gaze once more, a slight movement of her mouth, a near smile, showed him that she was grateful for his kindness. She glanced once in the direction that Johnny Montana had gone.

"I don't know if that would seem right," she

said, "me calling you by your first name."

"Well, I'd prefer it," he said, easing down beside her, holding the reins of all three mounts in his hand. The pack mule was contained by a lead rope tied to his saddle horn.

She thought him handsome, but not in the rakish way she had once thought Johnny Montana was handsome. The ranger had a soft, boyish face and crisp eyes that seemed forever shadowed under the brim of his dusty black Stetson. He had the raw-boned leanness of the land itself. She found both his speech and his manners to be pleasant.

"It's terribly warm, Texas," she said, patting the damp kerchief to her face.

"Well, maybe back where you come from," he said, with an easy smile. "But out here, I'd say this is just about normal. Now, when it gets so hot you have to put newspaper in the bottoms of your shoes to keep the soles of your feet from blistering, that's when it's considered warm."

She laughed slightly.

"Is it normal for Texans to tell such tall tales?"

"Oh yes ma'am. If us Texans couldn't swap stories, we might just as well all move to Kansas. Surely you have heard by now that everything in Texas is bigger and better and much improved over what the rest of the country has to offer."

He pushed back the brim of his hat far enough to reveal a sandy shock of hair and the crystal clear gray eyes, exposing a tender shyness that greatly appealed to her.

She thought that if this were another time, another place, they could easily have been two young lovers out for a day's ride.

He had been entertaining thoughts of her as well. She was pretty and good-natured, and did not complain. It was hard for him to understand how she could have ended up in such a mess.

A rustle in the distance drew their attention.

Johnny Montana, his gaze immediately fixed upon them, hurried his step to where the couple were sitting.

"Seems a man can't hardly do his duty in the bushes without someone trying to steal his gal. I turn my back and the first thing I know, you two are getting cozy with one another!"

Pete Winter flushed with anger over the accusation, but more so over the outlaw's foul manner. He leaped to his feet to confront the man.

"I've warned you mister about prodding me. Now you just back off!"

"Go ahead, Tex! Show me how tough you are! Prove it to the lady! Go on, whip me while I'm handcuffed!" It wasn't jealousy that motivated Johnny Montana — jealousy had nothing to do with it. All he hoped for was that the ranger would make a mistake, lose control, anything that might give him a chance.

Katie quickly pushed herself between the two men.

"Please!" she said, her eyes pleading with the angry stare of the lawman. Her fear was not for the outlaw. She knew that Johnny could be deceptive and vicious and that if the two engaged

143

one another in combat, Johnny might gain the upper hand.

"Please, no more violence!" She had placed her hand on the lawman's chest, a slight pressure of resistance, a pleading for him to refrain.

It was in that instant that he saw the band of Comanche riding toward them, the dust rising up from the flying hooves of their ponies.

"Get mounted!" he ordered. "We've got serious trouble coming!"

Johnny Montana saw them at almost the same instant.

"Lord!" he cried. "It's Indians!"

Pete Winter lifted Katie off the ground and onto the saddle with one powerful movement, slapped his Stetson across the horse's rump and shouted, "Ride full out, and don't stop for anything!"

Then, he bolted for his own mount. Snatching the lead rope of the pack mule in one hand, he whipped the ends of his reins over the shoulders of his mount and raked his spurs across its flanks to prod it into a dead run.

The outlaw was riding neck and neck with the woman directly ahead of the lawman.

The leader of the Comanche band saw the quarry bolt — like rabbits who have been spooked from their hiding, he thought with excited pleasure. *They can run, but to where?*

He *yiieed* a cry to the others and they bent their bodies low over the flying manes of their ponies.

Pete Winter glanced behind him and saw that the pursuers were closing the distance quickly. He

144

dropped the lead rope of the pack mule, hoping that its load of supplies might be enough to divert, or slow down the pursuit.

He saw the pack animal run for a short distance, slow, and then stop altogether.

He caught up to the lead, rode alongside the woman.

"Stay with me," he shouted above the wind and drum of hoof beats. She looked frightened as she clutched the reins in both hands. He could see that she was not a good rider. His own pace slowed in order to stay with her.

He glanced once more behind him. One of the warriors had dropped off and now stood holding the rope of the pack mule, but the others were still in full pursuit. Their ponies were tough, sure-footed and long-winded. He knew that there would be no way that they could outrun the Comanches. A quick tally proved there to be eight of them.

Ahead Johnny Montana was riding the big black, its hooves tossing clods of dirt high into the air. The ranger spurred his own horse to catch up. The Comanches were gaining steadily, in minutes they would be on them.

The fine, solid quarter horse he rode finally pulled alongside the outlaw.

"They're going to catch us!" the lawman shouted. The outlaw's features were grim. Just ahead was an old buffalo wallow, its muddy depression dry and cracked.

"Pull up there!" he shouted pointing to the edge of the wallow. "Now!"

To make sure the outlaw obeyed his command, Pete Winter drew his revolver and aimed it at Johnny Montana's face. The outlaw pulled back on the reins of the black and slid to a stop just within the depressed saucer of earth.

Pete Winter leaped from his saddle, put the barrel of the pistol to his horse's head and pulled the trigger. The animal dropped onto its side. The lawman then stepped quickly to Katie's animal, lifted her from the saddle and fired a second shot into the horse's brain. It fell next to the first one.

"What the hell are you doing?" cried Johnny Montana who was doing his best to control the panicky black.

"We need breastworks," the ranger shouted back. "Those Comanche braves catch us, we won't need these dern horses!" He jerked the Winchester from its boot and undid the saddlebags that carried the spare ammunition and revolver.

The swarthy renegade leader of the band of Comanches saw one of the whites shoot the two horses. It would be less of a victory. But still, there were scalps to be taken, coup to be counted upon the enemy.

The ranger handed over the spare pistol to Johnny Montana.

"You decide to use this on anything other than those Comanches," he warned, "you'll spend eternity right here!"

Grabbing the reins of the black, he tapped the forelegs of the animal causing it to kneel and then tapping its flank, it rolled over on its side.

"Katie, you come over here and lay down beside ol' Bo. Stroke his muzzle and he'll stay down like this out of harm's way. I taught him this trick for fun. Now, I'm glad I did."

She seemed paralyzed with fear. He took her gently by the arm and drew her near the fallen horse.

"Just like this," he said, demonstrating by placing her hand lightly over the black's nose. "Talking to him don't hurt any either. It's a good thing I taught him how to lay down rather than fetch wood," he said with an assuring grin.

"We'll need him when we get through taking care of these Antelope Eaters." She regained her wits and did as the lawman requested of her.

"You stay put, Bo, or those ol' Comanches will be having you for supper."

He quickly turned his attention back to where Johnny Montana had taken up position behind one of the dead horses.

"They ain't stopping!" he yelled.

"I can see that," said the ranger, dropping behind the second horse and sighting down the barrel of the Winchester. He squeezed the trigger and one of the warriors was snatched from the back of his pony.

He quickly levered another shell into the breech and fired a second time. A warrior slumped over but did not loose his seat.

"Hold your pistol fire until they get on top of us!" he warned the outlaw. "You won't hit anything with that until they're in close."

Pete Winter cranked off shot after shot hoping to stop the charge cold. One of his shots took the pony out from under its rider and sent the brave flying. The warrior tumbled along the ground, staggered to his feet, fell a second time, gathered himself up, and when he did, the lawman shot him through the chest.

The charging band pulled up suddenly, less than a fifty yards distance. Two of their band were killed, a third wounded. The sudden lull gave the lawman a chance to reload his Winchester. He looked up, and while doing so, saw the puff of smoke from the rifle of one of the warriors. In the same instant, something hot and painful slammed into his right shoulder.

The pain numbed his grip on the rifle and it dropped away. He grabbed at the jagged, bloody wound, realized instantly that it had shattered bone before exiting.

He saw the hopeful look on the outlaw's face.

"You've been hit pretty good, ranger."

He pulled his revolver from its scabbard with his left hand. It felt odd, unbalanced but not so much so that he could not cock it and aim it at the nose of the outlaw.

"You've got any ideas about this being you're lucky day, mister, you better dig yourself a hole and crawl down in it. Because if they don't kill you, I will."

The renegades had turned and ridden out of rifle range.

They made medicine.

"Two Robes and Long Lance are dead," said the muscled leader. "Small Man With Arrows suffers greatly from his wound."

"They have but one horse," replied another of the group. "We have them now, they cannot escape."

"Yes, let's avenge the death of our brothers!" cried another, the one holding the lead rope of the pack mule.

The wounded Comanche sat on the ground, rocking back and forth against the fire in his belly.

The leader stared off toward the distant buffalo wallow where the enemy lay.

"They have made us as few as them, and yet they suffer no dead, no wounded among them. This is a bad day to fight. If they are to die, let the heat and the lack of water and horses kill them!"

Without further comment, the short, stocky leader swung up upon the back of his pony and trotted away in the opposite direction of the quarry. Reluctantly, the others followed.

"Hey!" shouted Johnny Montana. "Those red bastards are turning tail — they're leaving!"

Pete Winter, struggling through the pain of his wound, watched the band of Comanches ride away. For now, they had survived the Comanche. The question now was, could they survive the rest of Texas.

Chapter Thirteen

It had taken the better part of a full day for the telegrapher to work up the nerve to tell U.S. Marshal Caleb Drew that he had been threatened into giving Eli Stagg a copy of the telegraph to be sent to the Texas Ranger station in Pecos.

"I think he must have gotten on Al Freemont's trail," the bespectacled little man admitted shakily to the lawman. "I seen him riding out right after Al left, and in the same direction."

"Why'd you wait so damn long to come and tell me?" asked the Marshal.

"Man said if I spoke a word about anything, he'd come back and cut off my head and put it in a sack. Said he'd take it down to Mexico and sell it as a souvenir. Said he could get fifty dollars for a human head. It was something I had to think about."

Caleb Drew knew that Al Freemont would be no match for a man like Eli Stagg. But, it had been another two days after that before he had a man to send after Freemont to warn him of the danger pursuing him.

When he got the wire that Al Freemont's body had been found three days out from Ft. Smith, he sat stunned.

"God damn it!" said the dispirited Marshal at the news the telegrapher carried to him. "That poor old man wasn't much worth a damn anymore, but he didn't deserve to be ambushed!"

Most days, being a Federal Marshal didn't mean too much more than having to be political with the right people. But, on days like this one, holding the position was about as appealing as falling down a well.

"Well, I don't have a soul to send after his killer, and even if I did, it'd be tough to catch up to him with so much of a lead." He reached in his lower desk drawer, found a bottle of bourbon. It was midday, but a drink seemed called for.

His mind mulled over the situation. There was no hard evidence that Eli Stagg had killed his deputy, but, he reasoned, it didn't take a detective to come to that conclusion.

Marshal Caleb Drew found himself silently cursing the situation. He absently fingered his own badge with one hand while holding the glass of bourbon in the other. He had played it safe, gotten political appointment, tried the best he could to do right by his men in the field. He considered himself a good man, a good politician, but deep within his soul, he knew he was not a lawman in the truest sense. Not a lawman like ol' Al Freemont had been a lawman.

He rode a desk and used a pen and attended *functions* where fried chicken and peas were served, and ladies gave him their opinion on such matters as Temperance and the Pythagoras Society.

He drank tea from little china cups and listened to piano recitals. That was what being a U.S. Marshal had meant for Caleb Drew.

Captain Ben Goodlow received the telegram from Ft. Smith:

Man I sent to meet your man in Ardmore, IND. Nations, has been found murdered. I believe the responsible party to be a man named Eli Stagg. He is a bounty hunter on the track of the two prisoners sent in your ranger's care. It is best for you to alert your man to the danger of encountering the impostor. U.S. Marshal Caleb Drew. Ft. Smith, Ark.

Ben Goodlow studied the wire grimly. Pete Winter and the prisoners had been gone for more than a week. He could only guess as to their present location upon the vast open country. He turned to a huge map tacked on his wall and studied it for a time trying to estimate exactly where the party would be.

Figuring their travel to be somewhere between twenty and forty miles a day, he could only guess that they would be within a hundred to one hundred and fifty miles of Tascosa, where he had last heard from Henry Dollar.

It was a long shot, but, if anyone could hope to locate the trio before they reached the Indian Nations, it would be the seasoned ranger.

Two fruitless days of checking with ranchers had brought Henry Dollar no closer to discovering who was behind the cattle rustling.

He had travelled to several of the ranches in the area, spoken with weathered men who eyed him suspiciously, said little, and seemed as

152

skittish as mustangs.

One man, a rancher by the name of Billy King, talked freely however.

"Up in this here country, Mr. Dollar, we tend to take care of our own matters. Always had to it seemed. Fought the Red Man, fought the squatters, fought the thieves. It ain't that you ain't appreciated, so much as it is you're an outsider. Lawman maybe, but still an outsider. Besides, you're just one feller and there's a whole bunch of them beef stealers runnin' round."

King was a man who spoke plainly and spoke the truth. Henry Dollar knew that whatever "bad business" was taking place around Tascosa was most likely going to be settled by men like Billy King.

Henry Dollar decided that his trip to Tascosa had been a washout. Except of course, for the matter of Josie Miller.

"Mr. Dollar," said Billy King as the ranger turned to leave. "Most of these fellers around here are good men. Independent maybe, but they have just reason. Don't judge our lot too harshly."

"I appreciate your time, sir," said Henry, touching the brim of his Stetson. "I believe the matter of cattle rustling around here will be resolved, one way or the other."

It had grown late by the time he had ridden back into town. As he rode past the office of City Marshal, Royal Curtiss was leaning the back of his chair against the adobe wall. The lumbering lawman came up with a start as soon as he saw the ranger on the buckskin.

"Hallo there, Dollar!" he shouted as he came waddling from his position, his bulk shifting with each step.

Henry drew back on the reins and waited for him to approach.

"Got this in earlier in the day," he said, holding out a piece of paper. "It's from your office down in Pecos." Henry took the paper and read it. A frown creased his features.

"Well, it looks as though you'll be leaving our fair town." He grinned and spat and placed his hands on his hips. The man was full of himself.

"I guess maybe the onliest one that's going to miss you around here is Mrs. Miller." The lawman's laugh was cut short at the sudden flash of the big Remington held in the ranger's hand.

"That kind of talk could get you killed, mister."

The effect was visible; the squatty bowlegs of Royal Curtiss buckled and he staggered back several steps in order to regain his balance.

His hands flew up in the air, and he cried: "Don't shoot me, mister — I don't want to be murdered!"

"Then leave me be, Marshal, or pull your piece!"

The florid face of the constable turned ashen, a mist of sweat banded his forehead. Henry Dollar watched as the man stumbled backwards across the street and disappeared into his office.

He touched spurs to the buckskin and rode out to Clave Miller's ranch.

She was standing there in the yard when he rode

154

up. Like the first time, only this time as though she had been waiting for him.

"I saw you coming," she said. "I knew it was you by the way you rode. I never saw a man ride the way you do."

He looked around the outfit.

"Where's Clave?"

"He's been gone since yesterday. He didn't say where. I can only guess that he's gone to Mobeetie again. He's been drinking ever since you left."

"Did he. . . ."

"No, he did not strike me or put a hand on me, but I would not have been surprised had he taken his pistol and shot me. He has been in a stew the whole time."

"I have to ride out," he said. *It was best just to say it,* he reasoned.

"Can I ask you why?"

"Received a wire just a short while ago, a friend needs my help. It can't wait."

"Not even until morning, Henry?"

"I reckon not, Josie. I wish it could be so."

"Can you wait long enough for me to put some food together for you?"

"Maybe just a minute or two."

"Climb down then and have yourself a smoke while I get some things prepared."

He waited for her, watered Ike at the tank, smoked a cigarette.

She came out of the house carrying a burlap bag, handed it to him and said, "There's enough there to last you two or three days."

He took it from her and tied it to his saddle.

"Henry?"

"Yes?"

"Will I ever see you again?"

"Well, I was hoping that maybe we'd have enough time to figure everything out," he said, removing his Stetson and running his fingers through his hair. "I guess plans don't always work out the way we'd like."

"That doesn't answer my question."

"I reckon it doesn't," he said, unsure of exactly what he should tell her.

"I don't want to say something I can't abide by in the long run."

"What does that mean?"

"It means I'd like to come back for you. I just don't know that it will happen."

"Because I'm married, or because of who you are?"

"Maybe a little of both."

They both felt the disappointment of circumstance.

"Then you must go," she said. "Go and decide whether or not to come back. I'll be here for you if you want me."

He kissed her gently, and for a moment, she put her arms around him and held him.

It had already grown late by the time he left Clave Miller's spread. As things would have it, he camped near the confluence of the Canadian and the Rita Blanca, the spot where he and Josie had had their picnic.

He built a small fire from some gathered dead-wood that had fallen from a few cottonwoods along the banks. He rubbed down Ike with handfuls of grass before putting on the hobbles and allowing the buckskin to graze.

Casting his bedroll several feet from the stream, he dug through the sack of victuals that Josie had prepared for him: fresh baked biscuits, drumsticks of chicken, a can of peaches, and a jar of but-termilk.

He ate hungrily and thought of her as darkness descended over the land. He thought about her, and he thought about himself. He lay back and looked at the stars and thought about how life had always been for him, how there were no fences in his life.

But, the old ways were passing, and, he wasn't quite as up to waking up mornings after spending all night on the ground and feeling like he'd been run over by a wagon. And trail grub was getting mighty gruesome.

The thought of bedding down every night in a sleigh bed with someone warm and special beside him seemed terribly appealing. So did the thought of good hot grub and conversation and sitting out of the evening and smoking a cigarette and feeling at peace.

He rolled up in his bedroll thinking that maybe after this matter of catching up to Pete Winter was over, he just damn well might ride on back up to Tascosa and see a woman he knew.

Something brought him fully awake. The night was as black as pitch, only the flowing waters made a sound. But, something had stirred him from his sleep and now he could feel the thump of his heart.

His hand eased silently for the big Remington that lay near his head. The fire had all but burned off, only a few embers winked in the darkness.

In the distance, a bolt of lightening splayed through the sky followed by the deep rumble of thunder. The buckskin whinnied its nervousness, the ears came alert.

The lawman moved silently away from his bedroll. Bolts of lightening continued to flash, momentarily casting the landscape in ghostly hues of light. He worked his way toward the small stand of cottonwoods near the river.

Drawing near the trees, the sudden flash of twin bolts illuminated the ground around him. In that instant, he saw the faces of men kneeling beside the trees.

They seemed like statues, their faces ghostly. They were there, and then they were gone. He threw himself to the ground, expecting at any moment a volley of gunfire from the trees.

The thick rumble of thunder rolled overhead, the air crashed with violence and slashed by electricity, and he was reminded of the sound and fury of war.

Working his way along the ground, he retreated back to where the buckskin was growing desperate, fighting against the hobbles. More lightening bolts, but this time, no faces appeared among the trees. *Where were they?*

He reached the buckskin just as the first drops of rain began to fall. Stroking the animal's neck, he managed to drop a rope over its head and tied the other end off to a fallen log.

The rain increased in intensity, knocking down the brim of his hat and soaking his skin. He found the saddle that lay by the bedroll and pulled the Winchester.

The seconds of waiting seemed eternal, but then, through the heavy pour of rain, he heard only what a man who lived by his wits would have heard: the snap of a twig not more than thirty feet away.

He fired blindly toward the sound. Someone cried out in pain. He immediately rolled several paces toward his left just as a flash of rifle fire sent a bullet whizzing past where he had been crouched.

He had counted three faces by the cottonwoods, but he knew there could be more. He figured them to be road agents.

He aimed the Winchester at the spot where he had seen the muzzle flash even though there was little chance the shooter would have held his position.

Most men were right handed. If a man shot and then rolled away from his position, he most generally rolled to his right.

Henry swung the barrel of the rifle a few inches to the left of the spot of muzzle flash. Before he could squeeze the trigger a second shot banged into the dark. The flash of light was directly at the point he had been aiming.

He squeezed the trigger immediately, too quickly for the shooter to move away. Something thudded to the ground.

"Little Ray, you get that sumabitch?" he heard a voice call out from somewhere to the rear of his position. Henry turned, laid the rifle down and drew his revolver. The voice was close.

"Kid, I am shot through the guts . . . the bastard shot me through the guts . . . blow his head off, Kid!"

Henry fanned the hammer of the Remington, the pistol banged six times. He could hear the *Kid* grunt and then, only the splattering of the rain sounded.

The ranger quickly ejected the shells from his revolver and reloaded. The wait seemed endless. The rain fell in hissing torrents, battered his hat, soaked his clothes, and he waited.

Waited like he had known Apaches to wait, silent and stock still.

The storm was marching away in the distant and eventually, the rain stopped altogether. Every muscle in his body was cramped from the damp coldness of night, but still he waited.

After the darkest hour, came the first light of dawn. It crept over the land, pushing back the shaggy shadows as it came. And when the light became enough, he saw, directly in front of him, not twenty yards distance, the body of a man. Sweeping his gaze in a wide circle, he saw another man slumped by one of the cottonwoods.

The third man was missing.

With caution he got to his feet, the cramped muscles unwilling to let him move too fast. He moved to the nearest body, examined the face, saw the homely but youthful features frozen in a mask of pain.

Moving to the man slumped near the tree, he felt a strange foreboding as he drew near. There seemed something familiar about the man, something about the clothes, the hat. When he tipped the man back to look at his face, he then knew what it was that had given him that dark feeling: Dead as dust from a shot through the neck that had bled him to death was Clave Miller.

"Damn," he muttered. In spite of the troubling revelation, the business at hand was unfinished. There was yet another gunman to be found.

Upon further inspection of the killing ground, he found a blood trail leading through the tall grass that flanked the stream. Checking the loads in his weapons, he followed it.

A half hour of trailing the blood smears brought him to the edge of where the bank dropped away several feet to the water. He saw the fresh tracks of boot heels in the soft ground leading down the bank and along the shoreline and curving out of sight around a bend.

He worked his way carefully down the bank and moved cautiously as he followed the trail. Just where the bank curved, he laid the Winchester down and drew his pistol. At close range, he preferred a pistol.

Stepping around the curve of the bank, he found what he was looking for.

The wounded man turned his head at the sound, saw the big man coming toward him, saw the revolver in the man's hand.

He closed his eyes and clutched at a place just above his belt buckle — a place that was sticky with blood. He saw the big man coming and closed his eyes and swallowed hard several times.

Henry Dollar saw that it was just another boy, like the first one, not much older than twenty and with the same familiar homely features as the first — he figured them to be brothers.

The kid was gut shot, his skin gone to gray from loss of blood. Henry had seen a lot of men in his time that had been gut shot and instantly he felt sorry for the boy, for the terrible agony such a wound can cause.

The boy's eyes fluttered open, came to rest on the large man standing over him. They were frightened, nervous eyes, eyes that spilled tears down the sides of his dirty cheeks.

The wound was bubbling blood between his fingers.

Henry slid his pistol into its holster. The boy was no threat and never would be again.

"It wasn't nothin' personal against you . . . mister," he said through gritted teeth. "Clave . . . he said . . . he said you was nosing around about the cattle rustling . . . said he wasn't going to be arrested for taking what he was entitled to take . . . said. . . ."

"Save your breath, boy. I know why you come. What'd he pay you to help ambush me?"

"Hun . . . hundred dollars, each. Me and Little Ray. Is Little Ray . . . dead?"

"He is. So is Clave Miller. Cold as ducks, and you're about to be. I guess you paid a dear price for one hundred dollars."

The boy coughed and cried out in pain.

"You want to make peace with the man upstairs, I'll give you some privacy. If you want, I'll carry a message to your kin or loved ones. I'll write it down and see that it gets to them sooner or later."

The boy wept. Henry rolled a cigarette and said, "Do you smoke, son?" And when he nodded that he did, the lawman put the cigarette to his lips and let him smoke it.

For a time, the boy seemed peaceful, absent of pain and fright. Henry knew that death was near.

"I ain't hardly lived at all," he said in a hoarse whisper. "I ain't never had a chance to be with a girl . . . won't never have no kids of my own. I ain't never even been out of Texas, mister."

Henry kneeled by the edge of the water, took his bandanna and dipped it in the stream. He laid it across the boy's brow.

"Any message you want me to carry to your kin?" asked Henry, knowing that the young man's time was drawing near.

"I have a ma over in Paris Flats . . . her name is Emilia Bright . . . if you wouldn't mind . . . tell her that her boys, Sandy and Little Ray was

163

killed in a stampede . . . I don't think she'd mind the lie . . ."

"I'll tell her son. You just lie back and rest now. I'll track on back and get a canteen of water and a blanket to ease your suffering."

"Mister . . . I don't know no prayers . . . Maybe you could say one for me?" Tears streamed down the boy's face.

The request was a difficult one. But, looking at the sad and pitiful face of the dying boy, it seemed one that could not be refused.

Henry removed his Stetson and held it to his side and cast his eyes to the blue peaceful sky.

"Lord, I'm not the one that should be representing this boy's case, but right now, I'm all he's got. It seems to me that he is paying for the error of his ways and he's been given about all he can handle. I don't think anyone would find it wrong to ask your forgiveness and ask that he be taken into your heavenly home. Amen."

The youth coughed once, caught his breath, looked up at the lawman and smiled.

"Mister?"

"What is it, son?"

"Could . . . could you stay with me until . . . until it's over?"

The lawman nodded.

"Sure. I won't go anywhere until it's over."

It was not a long vigil.

Afterwards, he closed the kid's eyes and folded his arms across his chest and rode away. There was no time to return and tell Josie what had happened. Instead, he stopped at the next ranch, owned by a fellow name of McTeal. He told the man the story, asked him to bury the men and to take word to Josie Miller that her husband was dead. Killed by a Texas Ranger. If things worked out right, he would return some day and explain it to her. But right now, he had no time.

Chapter Fourteen

The whistling wind cut across the plains sweeping sagebrush and sand before it. The stalking darkness found the trio camped within the old buffalo wallow.

Pete Winter could feel his strength oozing away from the hastily dressed shoulder wound. He fought the desire to close his eyes and slip into a painless sleep, knowing that was exactly what Johnny Montana was hoping that he would do. To lose consciousness would mean losing his prisoner, and more likely his life.

As soon as the Comanches had fled, he ordered the outlaw to replace the manacles on his wrists and ankles. Now he sat holding the pistol in his left hand in order to keep guard over the prisoner, a guard he knew he could not maintain for long.

"I need your help, Miss Swensen," he said against the rising sense of dread that was beginning to overtake him.

"You help him out, Kate, and it's the same as you putting a rope around our necks — both our necks. Leave him be. There's not a thing he can do. Soon's he goes under, we'll take that trick horse of his and ride away. We'll be free!"

She looked from one man to the other; from the dark smoldering eyes of Johnny Montana to the narrow, pain-filled eyes of the ranger.

"What is it you want me to do?" she asked,

knowing that if she did nothing, *they* would be free, her and Johnny. But she knew that she no longer wanted to be with the outlaw, no longer wanted to be on the run and fearful of being tracked down.

"Don't do it, Katie, I'm warning you! Ain't nothing going to save that boy if you don't help. Let it be!"

"No, Johnny! I'm through listening to you. I won't be party to letting him die!"

"You are a damn disappointment, girl!"

"What do you want me to do?" she asked the lawman.

"I need you to take my knife and cut some of those yucca stalks and help me build a fire, I need to try and cauterize this wound. I've lost about all the blood I can afford to."

She reached for the knife, when she did, Johnny Montana scrambled to his feet in spite of being manacled. His face was flushed with anger, his mouth full of curses for her.

His surge was stopped cold by the sound of the hammer being cocked on the Colt that rested in the lawman's left hand.

"You hold your water, mister, or I'll see that you are tried, convicted and sentenced right here and now!"

"You don't have the heart for it, boy!"

The shot exploded dirt between the toes of the outlaw.

"That's where you're wrong again, mister. That's where you are dead wrong! The next one goes through your brisket. Now burrow your butt back down in the dirt and stay there!"

Within a few minutes, Katie had cut several stalks, broken them in two, and struck several kitchen matches before the fire took hold.

"Now I need you to help me uncrimp some of these shells," he said, holding forth a handful of bullets. "I need the gunpowder from them."

Using his knife, they managed to dig the lead out of the bullets and pour the gunpowder into a tin cup. The effort was tedious and each movement caused the young ranger to wince in pain.

The outlaw, sitting in the shadows, watched and waited, sure that his time would come soon.

Finally, there seemed enough gunpowder in the cup to satisfy the lawman.

"Now, Katie, I want you to sprinkle that powder over the wound in my shoulder." She did as he asked, carefully making sure that she did not spill any.

When she finished, Pete Winter took her by the wrist.

"What I want you to do now is to take one of those burning stalks out of the fire and put it to this gunpowder. Keep yourself back from it as much as you can, protect your eyes, it'll flare up hot and quick."

She looked at him with an unwavering gaze.

"I'm hoping it will cauterize the wound and stop the bleeding. If not, I won't last the night. I'll most likely go under from pain when you light it. If I do, you're the only thing that stands between me and him," he said, nodding toward the outlaw.

"You know what his intentions are. Do you know how to use a pistol?"

She shook her head. "I've never had the need to fire one."

"It's easy," he told her, handing over the Colt. "You just point it like you would your finger, thumb back the hammer, and squeeze the trigger."

"I . . . couldn't shoot Johnny," she whispered, her eyes imploring him.

"No, I guess you couldn't," he said, leaning back against the saddle of one of the dead horses.

"But I guess if you can't find it within you to do so, you'll have to watch him kill me . . ."

She saw the eyes of the ranger flutter white, saw his head fall to his chest, saw him struggle to regain consciousness.

"It's time," he said. "I can't hold out any longer. Do it now!"

She reached into the fire and pulled out a burning stalk, hesitated for an instant and then touched its flame to the gunpowder on the wound. A *whoomp* of flashing white light burned into the night, into the wound, and she heard him moan once and slump over. She quickly poured water from one of the canteens onto the bloody dressing she had removed earlier and packed it against the cauterized wound.

She heard the rattle of Johnny Montana's chains, heard him scuttle to his feet.

"It's all over now!" he said.

She turned quickly to face him, the heavy weight

of the pistol in her hand reminding her of the lawman's warning.

"Don't," she said, raising up the Colt with both hands.

He paused for an instant, there in the light of the fire, his features knotted in anger.

"Girl, what has got onto your mind? Don't you see unless we take our chance now, we'll both be swinging from a hangman's rope in a few more days? Have you gone daft?"

"I won't let you hurt him, Johnny. You've hurt enough people and I didn't do anything to stop you. But I'm going to stop you from hurting *him.*"

"Don't let your heart get in the way of your head, woman. Hell, you fancy that boy, that's fine with me. But, I ain't going to let you or him bring me to a hanging."

She thumbed back the hammer of the Colt and the sound it made caused the outlaw to catch his breath.

"Whoa up, gal. Easy with that piece, it's liable to go off and blow a hole in ol' Johnny."

"Then get back before it does!" she ordered. The effect was visible as she saw him back away from the fire a step.

"You'd actually do it, pull the trigger on ol' Johnny," he said with astonishment. "I'll be damned if I can believe that."

"I'll do what I have to," she said. "If you get shot, it'll be because you want to as far as I'm concerned. You have a choice."

An uneasy silence settled between them.

"Tell you what," he said. "You let me get these chains off and have that horse, and I'll clear out — I'll be gone like the wind."

"Why would I do that?" she asked. "If I let you take the horse, we'd be stranded out here in the middle of nowhere. We might as well be dead."

"I'll ride to the nearest settlement and send help back for you. How will that be?"

"You'll more likely ride to the nearest settlement and rob the place, Johnny. I have no reason to trust anything you say."

His growing irritation was evident in his voice: "I've had my bad ways, Katie, but I ain't the sort that would just ride off and leave you to perish out here. Oh no, ma'am. That ain't Johnny Montana's way." He strutted back and forth beyond the fire as best as he could strut with the manacles on.

"I don't believe a word you say, Johnny."

"Well then, maybe you'll believe this. How long is it you think you can stand guard over that kid? How long before you have to close them pretty eyes of yours and go to sleep? What'd you think will happen then?"

She knew he was right. She was already bone-tired. She and the ranger would be at Johnny Montana's mercy if he got his hand on the pistol. There would be nothing to stop him from having his way.

He could see the wavering doubt in her eyes.

"You toss me the key, Katie, and let me ride off out of here on the black and send you help.

It's the only way you or him stand a chance. You do that and we'll all get what we want out of this thing. I'll be free, and you won't have to worry about me anymore."

As much as she dreaded the thought of being stranded, she knew that she could not hold out until the ranger regained consciousness. The wound had been a terrible one and he had lost a lot of blood. She could not risk falling asleep and letting Johnny get to the pistol.

"Well, what's it going to be, woman?"

She reached into the lawman's pockets and found the key to the manacles. She flung them the distance between her and Johnny.

"You unlock yourself," she said. "But, I swear to you, if you make any move this way, I'll pull the trigger. I wouldn't have to be much of a shot to hit you at this distance."

His grin revealed a row of even white teeth.

"You don't have to worry about that none, darling. All ol' Johnny wants is his freedom." He had the shackles off in seconds.

"Are you sure you don't want to come along with me, Kate? It will be some adventure, I promise you that, and a damn sight better than facing up to a hangman's noose."

His effort at trying to be charming no longer had any effect on her — quite the opposite.

"No, Johnny. I've gone as far with you as I am ever going to go. And, if you don't send back that help you promised, I won't be surprised."

He laughed, shook his head. "It's too bad you

have come to feel as you have about ol' Johnny. I always thought you were a woman of uncommon looks and up till lately, a good companion. But you never were much on grit."

He started for the black.

"Toss over the two other canteens," she ordered.

"Could be a long ways to water," he said.

"That's not my concern, you're the one with the horse. We'll be afoot. We'll need the water more than you."

Reluctantly, he did as she ordered.

"Go on," she said. "Go on and ride away from here and don't come back!"

"It ain't too late, darling. You can climb on board. I won't even hurt that boy lying yonder if you want to go with me."

She pulled the gun up high, aimed it at him.

"I'm losing patience with you, Johnny. Git before I pull the trigger."

She watched the smile fade from his face, saw the last of the arrogant appeal.

"Have it your way, girl. But looking at what I'm seeing now, I'd say you made a poor choice." He bashed the heels of his boots into the flanks of the black and rode off into the darkness.

She waited until she could no longer hear the thud of the black's hooves, until there was only silence. Silence and the low whistle of wind that sounded like the mournful wail of a lonely land.

She took the horse blankets and covered the ranger and herself. His face was feverish and damp and she poured a little more water from the canteen and dabbed his face with it.

The fire provided little heat and was nearly spent, so she scooped up dirt to put on it. Without the fire, Johnny Montana might have a hard time locating them if he decided to return.

Once the fire was banked, the blackness of the night surrounded her. She felt as cold and lonely and exhausted as she ever had. She knew the only thing that would permit their survival over the next few days would be whatever spare strength she could muster.

She lay down next to Pete Winter, and wrapping her arms around him for warmth, she pulled one of the blankets over her. Just before she felt the last ounce of strength leave her and sleep overtake her, she laid the pistol by her side.

Chapter Fifteen

Caleb Drew did his best to keep himself busy, but Al Freemont kept coming back to nag him time and time again. It was not that he felt particularly close to the old lawman, it was not that. Al Freemont was an irascible old cuss who had come to develop offensive manners and personal habits brought on mostly by his growing penchant for drunkenness.

Nonetheless, Caleb Drew knew his deputy to be a man who had spent the better part of his life upholding the law. And in spite of his own admitted shortcomings: "I ain't the best shot that ever was," he had often confessed, "And paperwork leaves me cold," Al Freemont was a man that would not shirk his duty, and did not, even on his final assignment.

"He always stuck pretty good," another deputy had said at hearing his fate. "Drunk or sober, happy or blue, Al rode whatever horse was given to him."

In spite of everything — old, drunken, busted down — Al Freemont still merited the praise and testimony of his fellow lawmen for having upheld his office and duties. Caleb Drew, sitting in the shaft of dusty light of his conventional office, realized that the murdered deputy had been twice the lawman that he himself was, and the thought nagged at him.

At first, when the haunting of Al Freemont had begun, Caleb Drew tended to inwardly justify his own situation as an administrator. His chief responsibility was to see that assignments were made, reports filed, payrolls met, correspondence with the appropriate authorities made, and so forth.

That was his job — to make sure the law got administered. But now, it didn't seem like enough.

He wore a badge and a cream-white Stetson hat, a string tie and a blue-steel Colt revolver . . . for all the world, he looked like a U.S. Marshal.

It seemed an illusion.

But still, he had refused to admit the truth to himself.

He had the command and respect of local businessmen, ranchers and politicians. He even had the ear of Judge Parker himself when it came to matters of legal advice. He had a good position in life, appointed by the President of the United States. He had a wife and dutiful children. Why risk it all because of some silly notion that he was a fake to himself and others? That was the question that Al Freemont's death had raised.

A question that begged an answer.

"I'm going to the Nations!" he announced to his assistant, Roy Stove.

"What fer?"

"I need to arrest a fellow."

"That's what us deputies are fer, Marshal," rebutted the assistant.

"Not this time. This is something special."

The assistant seemed confused, scratched a place

under his hat brim and snuffled through his nose.

"Don't seem right, Caleb, you doin' a deputy's work. Just don't seem right."

"It does to me, Roy," said the lawman, removing a holstered pistol from his desk drawer. It wasn't something he felt all that comfortable with, having never had a real need to use the thing. But, holding it now brought him a sense of himself and his mission.

"I ever tell you that before I became a U.S. Marshal," he said to the curious-eyed assistant as he strapped the gunbelt around his waist, "that I used to sell barbed wire?"

"No sir, you never did," replied Roy Stove.

"Yes sir, I sold a lot of barbed wire throughout this country. I was a successful salesman, made good money and had friends in high places. That's how I come to get this appointment — through well-placed friends of mine."

"Well, why in the world would you give it up to become a Marshal?" asked the deputy.

"I wanted to become a lawman. It was just something I thought I wanted to be." He took one of several Winchesters riding in a rack along the wall and two boxes of shells.

"Well, you look set fer bear, Marshal, I'll say that fer you. But, it ain't necessary you go out on a job yerself."

Caleb Drew started for the door but paused as he reached it.

"I know that you and some of the other deputies haven't thought highly of me as a lawman, not like Al Freemont was a lawman . . ."

Roy Stove started to wave a hand in protest, but Caleb Drew cut him off.

"No need to deny or discuss it," he continued. "Truth is, up until now, I haven't seen myself as much of a lawman. I reckon it's time that I see if I can uphold the law as well as I once could sell barbed wire."

"I reckon you just might, Caleb," said the deputy with a toothy grin.

"I don't know how long I'll be gone, or when I'll be back exactly," he told the deputy. "Just don't let your backside get too fond of my chair, and don't put any heel marks on the top of my desk. You do, and you'll have me to answer to." He stepped outside his office and headed toward the livery to acquire his horse.

Just walking down the middle of the street, well-heeled, with the Colt on his hip and the Winchester balanced in his hand, was beginning to make him feel like a true lawman.

Ardmore, The Indian Nations

She billed herself as THE YALLAR ROSE, and she was the largest soiled dove that ever escaped a gilded cage: three-hundred pounds of Chinese and Mexican with a face as round as a fry pan, arms as big as a miner's thighs, and feet so dainty that no one could understand how they held her up.

She plied her trade in the Black Moon Club on Second Street. It was the best low place in the Nations and every evening it was beset by the crashing of piano keys under the brown worn fingers of a Negro in a straw boater, blue smoke, the high-pitched laughter of parlor girls, and on occasion, the bang of gunfire.

The Black Moon Club was the sort of place that Eli Stagg knew he could cut the wolf loose in after a long hard ride. And when he spotted the Yallar Rose, he knew he had fallen into good fortune.

He saw her sitting in a chair that seemed lost beneath her bulk, talking to a pair of miners, a cowboy and an Indian. It did not deter his attraction.

"I am Al Freemont and I'm a Federal Marshal," he announced, over the protesting glances of her court. He pulled the badge out of his pocket and showed it to her, to her audience as well. They suddenly found other places they thought they should be.

She turned her attention toward him. Aside from the powdered face and cheeks rouged as red as apples, she had eyes as black as a horse-thief's heart.

Upon giving the mountain man the once over, she cried out in a high thin voice: "Waugh, did you come here to arrest me or to screw me?" And then she laughed in a way that shook her entire body and threatened to bust out the sides of the velvet dress she was wearing.

He knew right off he was consorting with the devil. He liked everything about her.

"Ain't never seen no woman like you," he said.

"That's 'cause there ain't no other woman like me, Marshal."

"That's a fact. How about splitting a bottle of champagne?"

"Well gosh and be damned, if you ain't the one," she said. The red parting of her lips showed that her teeth had seen better days.

He ordered up a bottle of house champagne and blew the cork clear to the ceiling. It bubbled out of the bottle and spilled over his fingers as he poured it into glasses.

She drank the first glass down in a gulp, and so did he. He poured another and she did the same.

"What's a high-toned woman like you doing in the Nations?" he asked.

"Same as everyone else, I just wound up here on my way to someplace else."

"Well have another drink and let's talk business."

"Exactly what kind of business did you have in mind, honey?"

"The kind I believe you are selling."

"You ain't exactly a romantic man, I can see that," she said, reaching for the bottle of champagne and refilling her glass.

"And you ain't exactly somebody's bride," he said, foregoing the glass and tipping the bottle directly to his mouth.

"How much you willing to pay for the Yallar Rose?" she asked.

"Well honey, if you ain't chargin' by the pound, I reckon I can pay the freight. How much?"

"Judging by the dust on your britches, I'd say

it's been a time since you had a woman," she said. "I reckon a man whose gone so long without a woman ought to be willing to pay thirty dollars for the privilege of being with the Yallar Rose."

"Thirty dollars."

"There's cheaper around," she said. "But they ain't never going to do for you what the Yallar Rose will."

"I'll give you ten, not a cent more."

"Honey, like I said, you ain't much of a romancing man. Make it twenty and let's go."

He reached in his pocket and peeled off twenty dollars and handed it to her.

"This sure better be somethin'."

"Don't you worry none, mister, it'll be a thing of wonderment."

The next morning, he felt as though his head had been busted in from all the champagne. The Yallar Rose was a sonorous pile of flesh that weighed the springs of the mattress all the way to the floor.

He got dressed and rifled through her clothes until he found the twenty dollars he had given her the night before.

"Damn fool woman must've thought I just fell off a hide cart to think she'd clean me for twenty skins," he said to himself, stuffing the money back into his pocket.

The next thing he needed to do was report in at the local law office, announce himself as Al Freemont, Federal Marshal and see if any Texas Rangers had showed up carrying two prisoners.

If they had not, he'd just bide his time until they did.

He clumped down the stairs and saw the bartender sleeping atop the bar, curled up like a baby with his knees pulled up.

A cold morning light was filtering through the windows and the place was as silent as a graveyard.

He stepped outside into a muddy street that sucked at his boots as he walked. Sometime during the night a hard rain had fallen.

The town itself looked rotted and ready to fall down. He'd see the town law, have breakfast, and then just wait.

Chapter Sixteen

Pete Winter awakened from a fitful sleep; it felt to him like he had gone on a long and perilous journey. Waking up was both disappointment and surprise.

Katie Swensen pressed a canteen to his lips and the swill of water assuaged his dry lips and tongue. He swallowed and coughed and fell back into that deep dark place of unconsciousness.

She repositioned the horse blanket over him, wondered what hour it was. The night sky was indigo, the land hidden in blackness. She was trying to fall asleep herself again when she heard the call of wolves, their howl high and mournful. The dead horses were attracting their attention.

Reluctantly, she took the knife and cut more stalks and rebuilt the fire. She could hear something moving about beyond the circle of light, could hear sounds that threatened her nerve. But her resolve was clear: she would not let anything come into camp.

She held the ranger's pistol in both hands and cocked the hammer, just as he had shown her.

The growls and snarls drew nearer. She thought that she saw a shadow of something move just beyond the light. She aimed the pistol, holding it as steady as she could, and pulled the trigger. The roar of the shot echoed off into the night, and whatever it was that had been out there had retreated — at least for the time.

The silence that followed the gunshot caused her a deep sense of isolation. The imposing darkness, the threat of unseen creatures stalking the encampment, the severely wounded lawman next to her side — all were the source of a sense of dread for her.

She had resolved, however, that she would not let death come easy, either for her or the ranger.

She fought sleep to maintain a vigil against the stalking predators. Whenever they came too near, she fired the pistol and they scattered. Whenever the lawman stirred from his feverish sleep, she gave him water. Whenever the fire began to flag, she fed it more yucca stalks. She would not just let "it" happen.

If the lawman died, she told herself, then it would not matter what happened to her. She knew that she could not make it across this open country alone. She would save one bullet, just in case. If death reached her, she decided, it would reach her by her own hand and not that of another person, or another thing.

She checked the lawman's wounded shoulder several times. The cauterization had worked, the bleeding had been stopped. She did not know if it would be enough. He seemed so young, the face of a boy in repose.

She stroked his face and held his hand and thought of songs she had sang as a girl and sang them to him in a low soft voice that, at times, was drowned out by the wind or the cry of the wolves.

She turned her eyes heavenward and watched for shooting stars on which to say a wish upon. There were none. Slowly the constellations, some that she had learned as a schoolgirl, passed in slow rotation in the vast night sky.

Something warm touched her face and she awakened to it. It was the rising sun, warm and gentle. Tears spilled from her eyes from the relief and joy that she was still alive. She had fallen asleep next to the ranger, the pistol still gripped in her hand.

A moment's joy turned suddenly to a moment's fear as she remembered the wounded man's condition throughout the night.

She quickly checked him. His breathing was now even and his skin was cool to the touch once more. The fever had broken. He stirred to her touch. His eyes opened and his mouth turned up into a smile.

"Katie," he whispered in a dry, weak, voice. He struggled to sit up.

"Don't thrust about so much," she cautioned him. "It's alright. You had a fever in the night, but it's broken."

He saw her tears, moved his hand to touch them.

"I'm alright," she said. "I guess I'm just happy."

He could feel the dull ache in his shoulder, but the worst of the pain seemed to have passed. He looked around him, remembering.

"Katie, Johnny's gone!"

"Yes. I let him go. He rode out last night." She saw the look of confusion in his face.

"I had to let him go, he would have killed you the minute I fell asleep. There just wasn't any way I could stand guard over both of you the whole night."

He nodded. "It's alright," he said. "I reckon if he got caught once, he'll get caught again."

"Pete, he took the black. We're alone out here."

"I know."

"We've still got two canteens of water," she said. "I wouldn't let him take the water."

"That's a point in our favor," he grinned feebly. He knew immediately that the chances were slim to none. But, she had done the right thing, the only thing, that she could have. She had saved the two of them, and that in itself was hope of a sort.

"We need to eat," he said. "If we're going to walk the rest of the way across these staked plains, we need to eat."

The mention of food caused her to realize how hungry she was. But how were they to eat when all their supplies had been captured by the Comanches the day before?

"But what?" she asked.

"We've got them," he pointed to the dead horses.

"Pete . . . I couldn't. . . ."

"You will," he said. "Horse meat is good red meat, Indians eat it all the time. I've eaten it myself. Cooked right, it ain't much different than

186

beef. Can you build another fire?"

She nodded, reluctantly.

He waited for her to cut and gather more stalks before moving, with a great deal of effort, to one of the dead horses. Cutting from the haunches, he managed to slice out two fair-sized slabs of meat.

Spearing the meat and turning it slowly over the fire, the "horse steaks" were soon ready for tasting.

"You go first," she said.

He cut a slice from it and chewed on it, carefully avoiding its heat. It wasn't as tasty as he told her it would be, but he made a face like it was.

"It could use a little salt and pepper," he said, with a shy grin, "but it'll do."

Reluctantly she followed his example. She chewed in silence for a time, not giving any indication as to what she thought of the horse flesh.

He chewed while watching her. Waited.

Finally, she finished a piece and said: "It's not too bad."

"See."

"Well, I suppose as long as I don't think of its source . . ."

"Heck," he said. "Comanches will ride a horse until it's played out and then eat the dang thing for supper. They get double use out of the ponies that way."

"I hear they eat dog, as well," she commented by making a face.

"Well now, dog is a different thing altogether,

187

in my book it is," he said. "But, I suppose if a body got hungry enough. . . ."

"Not me," she shuddered. "This is as far as I'd go."

"Don't be too sure," he teased.

They ate until they could eat no more, washing down the taste with careful amounts of water.

"We have to be real careful from here on out," he suggested. "I know that there is water out there somewhere, but just exactly where, I'm not sure."

"I understand."

The effort of preparing the meal and eating it had left him tired.

"Let me rest just for a minute and then we must get started."

"What are our chances, Pete?"

He had not been fully prepared for the question. It was one that he had been mulling over ever since he had awakened. Without horses, and with a limited supply of water, and with his wounds, the land was even more dangerous to them now than it had been. But, he reasoned, it was not an opinion that needed sharing right at this point.

His gaze searched the open plains before them; he saw nothing that offered him hope.

"Well, it's most likely we'll happen across water. And there are antelope and rabbits and deer, so most likely we'll get a chance at meat. I'd say, we got just as good a chance as anybody else," he said.

He saw a flicker of doubt in her eyes, saw the corners of her mouth drop in resignation.

"In other words," she said, "we're in bad shape."

He had to admire her grit.

"I suppose that's one way of putting it. But, I'm not ready to cash in my cards just yet."

He stood to his full height, ignoring as much as possible the pain in his shoulder.

"I look at it this way," he said. "We still got weapons, we got water, and we got our feet. There's nothing out there except land. We walk across enough of it, we're bound to get to somewhere."

His courage offered her reason for hope. She found herself wanting to hold onto him, wanting to put her arms around him and gather in his strength for her own.

"Do you know how to weave?" he asked.

"Some."

"Good, then go and cut a fist full of those yucca leaves and I'll show you how to weave them into a hat. You'll need head covering — this sun can get intense."

He helped her with the project and when she finished, she put it atop her head.

"You look like a Chinese maiden," he said.

She curtsied and said: "I do not."

It caused them both to laugh.

"Strap the extra pistol on your hip," he told her. She did so.

They each took a canteen and he carried the Winchester.

"We'll head that way," he pointed at an oblique

189

angle toward the direction of the sun.

"Mormon Springs is in that direction according to my map." He did not say that Mormon Springs lay fifty miles in that direction. He did not want to dishearten her. Nor did he want to think of this nearest town in terms of so many miles. From here on out, he reasoned, it would be one step at a time, one foot in front of the other.

"You ready?"

She nodded her head.

"Just a minute," he said after the first few steps. She watched as he sat down and knocked the heels off his boots.

"These things weren't built for walking," he explained. "I walk too far in these, my legs will coil up like snakes."

Chapter Seventeen

He had ridden the black until it started to falter. Begrudgingly he dismounted and began to walk, trailing the black behind. Half a horse seemed far better than no horse at all in a hostile land.

How long he had walked, he could not determine, but when the first buildings of Mormon Springs appeared, wavering in the distance through the rising heat of the prairie sod, he realized that his luck was still holding.

It was a town of clapboard houses, adobe buildings, and dirty canvas tents.

He found a livery. It was run by a pudgy faced man with a cockeye and a bowl haircut. The man looked to be a half-wit.

"Mistur," the half-wit said, "Yore horse looks worn out."

"Naw, he's not wore out. I just been running races with him and he's lathered is all."

"He a racer?"

"Best there is."

"Don't look like a racer."

"This here is a special horse, friend. Does tricks. He can run and do tricks, too."

"Dang."

"Wanna see?"

"Shore."

Johnny Montana tapped the forelegs of the black making it kneel down, and then slapped the flank until it rolled over on its side.

"He plays dead," said the outlaw. "All you got to do now is rub his nose and he'll stay like that until you make him get up."

"Dang!"

"Taught him that myself."

"Dang and double dang!"

"I'm teaching him other things too. Like, to count."

"No?"

"Yes sir. Trouble is, I have to sell him."

He saw the man's eyes grow wide with interest.

"You goin' to sell a smart horse like that?"

"Afraid so. Anyone with good sense would want him. I reckon I'll sell him easy."

The half-wit was thinking so hard it wrinkled the skin on his forehead and around his eyes.

"How much you askin' for yore horse, mistur?"

The outlaw continued to stroke the black's nose, then, finally tugged on the reins until he rose and shook the dust from his hide.

"Well, ordinarily I wouldn't take less than a thousand dollars for him."

The half-wit whistled through parted teeth.

"But, seeing as how I'm in a desperate fix, I'll take a hundred dollars, and maybe a fresh mount in exchange, for I do need me a horse to ride you understand."

"Taa . . . a hundred dollars is a lot of money, mistur."

"Not for a trick horse it ain't. Not for a racer. You can make that much back in a single race.

Hell, this here animal is as fast as the wind. Ain't nothing can beat him. You don't want him, that's your business. I reckon he'll sell fast enough. Just that you look like a good fellow. I'd prefer to see you have him."

"All I got is sixty dollars. And, I'll give you my best mare. That blaze-faced roan over there in the stall."

Sixty dollars wasn't much and neither was the mare, by the looks of her. But, the black was wore out and so was he. Hungry and wore out and he needed a drink.

"Everybody in this town as shrewd as you?"

"Don't know, mistur. You want to trade?"

He put the saddle on the mare while the half-wit counted out the money — money he had pulled his shoe and sock off to get to.

As far as the half-wit was concerned, life had never been so sweet. He had traded the man a soft-mouthed mare and sixty dollars for a trick horse. And, one that could race, too.

Dang!

Johnny spent a dollar on dinner and another on whiskey. And when the whore asked him, he spent another on her.

Afterwards, he slept through the heat of the afternoon in the whore's tent. He had to give her another dollar to let him do so.

"I'll be gone by dark," he said. She did not quibble or raise a fuss. Two dollars was damn near a fortune — especially in the middle of the day.

Later, he arose, went to the mercantile and bought a pistol for five dollars and a shotgun for ten. He paid fifty cents for shells.

The dream he'd had sleeping in the whore's tent had disturbed him. He was drowning in a river, and Katie and the ranger were holding him under the water, laughing all the time.

By the time he mounted the mare, he had decided what he needed to do, where he needed to go, and who he needed to kill.

Henry Dollar arrived in Mormon Springs two hours after dark. It was a sleepy little village except for its barking dogs. The buckskin's hooves spanked up dust as he rode down the street. He had ridden through the town once before, several years previous.

It proved to be like a lot of Texas frontier towns: cautious to strangers; no local law; and a known gathering spot for hard cases. Mormon Springs was just the sort of place that made it necessary for the state of Texas to hire men like Henry Dollar to wear a badge.

Unless he missed his guess, Pete Winter and his prisoners would pass through this town, if they hadn't already.

He reined in at a small cantina with adobe walls and oilskin windows that leaked yellow light. He hoped for a meal and something to cut the dust from his throat.

A sleeping Mexican lay curled up in front of the doorway, his blanket a tattered serape.

" 'Scuse me, señor," he muttered as he stepped over the prostrate form and entered the cantina.

The air was warm and stale like old cigar smoke and beer and sweat. A few dour faces took notice of the stranger's entrance.

He had been a lifetime reading faces. Those he saw now offered him no comfort. They were all Mexican, all hard-eyed and suspicious of his presence. But he was too hungry and thirsty to give a damn.

He moved to the bar, ordered tequila. Tequila was safer than whiskey in a place like this. He had known lots of places whose whiskey was little more than a barrel of alcohol with a plug of tobacco thrown in for color and rattlesnake heads for taste. Some called it Old Tose, he called it poison.

He put salt on his thumb, licked it, and downed the tequila. It warmed him through and through and took the edge off his weariness.

"Another, señor?"

The barkeep was swarthy, had a bad eye and worse breath. A bone white scar ridged his cheek. It was the sort of face that had seen some hard and pitiful things.

"No thanks, amigo. I've not yet et. What's the chance of getting some beef and beans?"

"Si. Mamacita," he called. A short squat woman appeared from behind a curtain at the rear of the cantina. She looked haggard, with oily black hair that was woven into braids. The man spoke to her in Spanish. The ranger understood that she was being told to go and prepare a meal and bring it to him. She shuffled away without a glance or a word.

"She bring you beef and frijoles and some tortillas real soon, señor," said the barman.

"Gracias, amigo."

He searched the room for a place to sit, saw one in the far corner.

There was little more sound in the room than the sound of expectant men breathing and the ring of his spurs as he moved to the chair and table.

He thought he could almost hear the ticking of the watch in his pocket as he waited for the woman to come with the food.

Someone moved in the recesses of the shadows. A woman, but not the same woman the Mexican barkeep had spoken to.

The light in the room was dim, as she neared his table he could see well enough to realize that she was a white woman. She had the gaunt features of someone in poor health. She was not young and even by frontier standards, she was not attractive.

She stopped there in the light, where it was best in order to give him a good look at her.

"How 'bout some fun, mister?"

"I'll pass."

"A drink, maybe?"

He nodded to the barman to bring the woman a drink.

"Whiskey," she said.

"You and me could have us a good time," she said. "Don't get many white men in here, but you're the second one today."

"Young handsome boy? A lawman, maybe?"

"Don't think so," she said, raising the glass of amber liquid to her mouth. She held it there a long full second before drinking it in a single swallow.

"You a lawman?" she asked.

"I'm looking for a friend of mine. He'd be with two others — a man and a woman."

"No, this fellow was by himself." She made a snuffling sound through her nose. Her attempt at smiling revealed several discolored teeth.

He felt disappointed that the man had not been Pete Winter. It would have been too lucky a circumstance.

"My name's Janey," she told him. "What's yours?"

"It doesn't matter."

The fat Mexican woman returned carrying a plate of food and sat it in front of him. The prostitute eyed the plate.

"Tell your woman to bring another plate of this," he said to the bartender, shoving the food toward the whore.

"You look like you can stand a meal."

She swallowed hard, turned her attention briefly to the dark curious faces around the room.

"Look, mister. You wanta buy me, that's fine. And, it ain't that I don't appreciate the offer. But . . . Migelo, he don't like me to waste my time socializing with the trade. It don't make no money."

"A man like that don't sound like much of a

man, sis. But, it's your choice." He reached for the plate, but she suddenly sat down in the chair across from him and gathered it in.

Her movements were quick and greedy as she spooned in the warm beans and slashed at the slab of beef.

He rolled himself a cigarette and looked away while she ate. It seemed to him too hard a thing to do to watch her hunger.

Her hands shook as she swiped up the juices left on the plate with the last of the tortillas and worked it in her mouth.

"I'll say this for white trade," she said, a sheen of grease staining her chin. "They can be generous almost to a fault. That fellow that was through here earlier paid me a whole dollar just to sleep awhile in my tent. Course, he paid me for other things too."

He wasn't interested in her business, and when brought his own meal, he ate it in silence. She watched him eat, seemed to study him until he finished.

He made a cigarette and smoked it. Still, she sat there observing him.

"I thought your man didn't like you wasting time," he said finally.

"He don't. He catches me . . ." She rubbed the side of her face where he could see the dark tracing of an old bruise under the powder.

"Come on over to my tent, mister. I'll let you have me for free, you want. Consider it a trade for the meal."

"Sorry, sis. I've got things to do."

"You don't think I'm pretty enough?"

"Let's just say I've ridden a long way and not in the mood and leave it at that." It seemed enough to satisfy her.

"Well, you change your mind before you leave town, my tent is just down the street from here. You ask anybody and they'll tell you where Janey's tent is at . . ."

There was a disturbance near the door.

Several men entered at once. She said, "It's Migelo!"

They were Mexican, wearing broad hats and big spurs and pistols high on their hips. They weren't town Mexicans. They moved straight to the table where he sat with the woman.

He could smell the dust and sweat of their clothes.

The big one in front eyed the woman first, then him.

"You with this man, eh?" he said.

"Just talking some business is all," she said, pushing her chair back from the table.

"He want to buy you, eh?" The Mexican eyed the two empty plates, the two empty glasses.

"No," she said. "We was just talking is all."

"You talkin' business with my woman, eh gringo?"

Henry Dollar pushed back from the table and stood facing them.

"Don't care for your tone, señor. Don't care for your manners, either. A man that would see

199

his woman sold to other men ain't much in my book. Pardon."

He stepped past the Mexican, walked to the bar and dropped two silver dollars on it. The sooner he made his leave the better for everybody. The Mexican was looking for trouble, he wasn't.

He heard the hard smack of flesh on flesh, heard the woman cry out, turned in time to see her falling to the floor, saw the Mexican standing over her, saw the satisfaction in their faces.

He dropped the flap of the duster back over the butt of his pistol.

"You leave up, mister."

The Mexican turned, his dark gaze coming to bear on the lawman.

"Hombre, you better go on while you can, eh?"

It was a joke, a game with them, the violence, the inflicting of pain. The frontier left some men idle, and others mean.

There was no time. The blow struck him from behind and across his shoulders. He heard the breaking of wood as he staggered. And suddenly, he was being pummeled from every side.

He swung a hard right fist that struck flesh and bone, and another that hit the softness of gut. But, for every blow he gave, he received many in return. And once down, they began to kick him.

In the final fading awareness, he could feel them stripping him of his guns and belt, they were lifting him, carrying him somewhere. He was dropped to the ground and he tasted dirt in his mouth, dirt and blood. Then the darkness came.

He came to with a jerk, still feeling the fists and boots driving into his body. The pain shot through his ribs and his head felt as if it would explode.

He opened the eye least swollen as much as he could and a stab of light caused him to wince.

"Stay quiet, mister." It was the woman's voice — the prostitute. He saw her in the smear of light, the unattractive face, the thin body. She sat near him in the muted light coming through the tent.

His throat was parched, he swallowed away the dryness, struggled to sit up. She helped him.

"Migelo and the others worked you over pretty hard," she said. "You're all beat to hell."

It was news she did not have to announce. He worked his arms; they were sore and bruised. At least a rib or two felt broken. He had no desire to look in a mirror, he could feel the damage to his face, he didn't need to see it.

"Didn't know you was a lawman," she said. "Neither did they till they saw the badge you was wearing. Likely they would have killed you otherwise."

"Surprised they didn't," he muttered through swollen cracked lips.

"Migelo said killing a lawman would just bring more. He wasn't interested in that. They stole you blind, though. Even took your horse. Rode out. Probably won't come back until after they figure you're gone."

"This your tent?" he asked, looking around. "This the one you wanted me to come to?"

201

"I guess I got you here after all," she said with a slight smile that hid her poor teeth. He saw the bruise on her cheek where the Mexican had slapped her.

"Yeah, I reckon so," he said, but unable to smile back.

"You want whiskey? I've got some whiskey."

He nodded and she poured him some in a tin cup. It hurt like hell but seemed to help.

He worked a hand down inside his boot, found the folded paper money he kept there and handed it to her.

"I need you to do me a favor."

She stared at the money.

"I need you to go buy me a pistol, two if you can. And, find me a doctor if there is one in town."

She didn't move.

"Don't worry, sis. I ain't going after your man, I've got other business needs tending. You go on and do as I say, I'll make it worth your time."

She turned to go.

"Leave the whiskey, eh?" She handed him what was left in the bottle.

She returned shortly with a man who had a whiskey nose and wore a once white shirt without the paper collar.

"Doc Bitters is who I am. Who are you?"

"Doesn't matter."

"Janey told me you was stomped, mister," the man said, leaning over to inspect the cuts and bruises on his face. "I'd say you was stomped pretty good."

202

"Fix what you can."

He sat patiently while the physician bound up his ribs. Bitters checked his scalp for cuts as well. After he had finished, he stood and said, "It's about all I know how to do for you," and handed him a small blue bottle with a cork in it.

"This is laudanum. Take a taste now and then for the pain, but don't overdo it. It has a way of making you crave it."

The physician looked at the woman, then back at him.

"Don't worry about the charges, Janey's offered to work it off. Lord knows that Janey's the best this town has to offer. Loneliness has a way of affecting us all."

The man made his departure.

She handed him a weighted burlap sack. "It's all I could find to buy," she said.

He took out a Schofield pistol that weighed as much as a brick, and a small Colt Lightening .38 caliber revolver with pearl grips. There was a box of shells for each as well.

"They cost me twenty dollars, here's the rest of your money."

"You go on and keep it," he said.

"No. You'll need to buy a horse. Don't you remember I told you they took your horse, Migelo and his bunch?"

"Why the generosity, sis?"

"You bought me a meal and stood up for me with Migelo. It's more than most men would have done."

He nodded, stood with great effort, and took the bag with the pistols. He turned at the flap of the tent.

"There a livery in town?"

"Not far up the street. Don't let ol' Crazy Jess cheat you. He looks half-witted, but he's as smart as a mule."

He gave her one last look before leaving her tent. If her looks would have half matched her heart, she would have been a beauty.

He found the stables three blocks north of the woman's tent. A man with a slab face sat out front, whittling a stick and whistling through his parted teeth. He looked up from the tip of the stick and observed the hitched gait of the stranger.

"I need a horse." The man looked as though he had fallen off a roof and landed on a pile of lumber. The face was all bruised, and it was plain to see he favored his right side.

"Oh, you must be that feller that was whupped in Lacy's Whiskey Tent last night. Whole town heard how you was whupped."

"I've got two pistols in this sack, and shells for them. I'm not in the mood for conversation." The threat was enough to cause the man to fold up his pocket knife and lift himself out of his chair.

"Horse, eh?"

"Got several you might be interested in, come on inside."

The lawman nodded.

He followed the slab-faced man into the dim

cool interior of the stables.

The man led him to a stall that contained a roan, but it was plain to see the horse was old and not much good for a long ride.

"Show me another."

The next stall contained a small gray. Before he could speak, the slab-faced man said, "Naw, she's too little for a big man like yourself. She'd give out in twenty miles."

He found a dun in the next stall and the dun nickered at their presence.

"How much?" asked Henry.

"Need a hundred dollars for him," said the slab-faced man.

"Don't have a hundred, I'll give you sixty."

"Couldn't take sixty, mister. Anybody can look at what a fine animal he is and see that I couldn't take sixty." The ranger was already looking at the other stalls, saw the black, moved to where the black had lifted its head over the gate.

"What about this one?"

The man shook his head with an exaggerated waggle.

"Couldn't sell that horse, mister. That's a racer and a trick horse."

The stableman watched as the stranger moved closer to the black's stall, moved closer and said, "Lead this one out."

"Already told you, he ain't for sell, that one."

The cold stare of the man caused the stableman to swallow the rest of his argument. He led the black out into the outside light.

205

Henry saw the patch along its neck, knew that it was Pete Winter's black — the one he had taught to lay down on command.

"Where'd you get this animal?"

"A feller brought him in yesterday."

"What sort of fellow?"

"Thin man, dark. Looked like he could be a gambler, maybe. Said he won money racing the black. Said he was teaching the black how to count. Don't see how, though. All I can do is get him to lay down. Can't get him to count."

"You know if this fellow is still around town?"

"Don't reckon so, I saw him riding out just past evening."

"Which way?"

The man thumbed the air toward the west road.

"Throw a saddle on the dun."

"I though you said you didn't have but sixty dollars?"

"I'll write a chit guaranteed by the state of Texas for the rest."

The man scratched his forehead. "I dunno . . ."

"It's either that, or take the sixty." The man saw the stranger retrieve one of the pistols from the sack and load it from a box of shells. The demonstration was obvious in its purpose.

When the stranger stuck the pistol in his waistband, the slab-faced man saw the badge pinned beneath the duster. Half watching over his shoulder as he saddled the dun, he saw the man load the second pistol and place it cross wise from the first in his waistband.

"Reckon you're after the feller that sold me the black, eh?"

The cold stare caused the stableman to step backwards.

Chapter Eighteen

Eli Stagg had stayed around the Nations for three days waiting for the Texas Ranger and Johnny Montana and the woman to show. He was nearly tapped out of funds, including the money he had taken off the murdered deputy.

The Yallar Rose had come looking for him and professed her love if only he'd return the twenty dollars he lifted off her. He bargained her into a three-course dinner instead, and over the next seventy-two hours did his best to use up his poke on whiskey, food, and a buggy ride to take her into the country for a picnic. She ate two whole chickens, and so did he.

Now he was broke, and the Yallar Rose had made herself scarce and the Nations was starting to stink too much of civilization as far as he was concerned.

The local lawman was a fellow by the name of Cherokee Tom, a half-breed who held the appointment of city marshal. The first two days that Eli Stagg had been in town, Cherokee Tom had been on a scout for some desperados that had stolen a wagon and a team of horses. The desperados turned out to be two drunken Choctaw Indians who stole the wagon rather than walk. They explained it to Cherokee Tom: "Why should us injuns walk when there was a perfectly good wagon and horses that nobody was using."

Tom had made them return the rig to its owners and promise that they would either stay sober from that time forth, or steal their transportation out of his jurisdiction. He had no faith that they would do either.

When he arrived back in Ardmore on the afternoon of the third day, he got word quick that there was a federal lawman in town. Cherokee Tom got curious.

Eli Stagg sat in the NATIONS BAR sulking over a warm glass of beer when Cherokee Tom walked in.

The bounty hunter took in the appearance of the lawman the moment he entered: a hard-looking fellow, face as sharp as a raven, black hair like one, too. A dandy dresser though, especially the tall crowned hat with the rattlesnake headband.

The bounty hunter noticed the pair of ivory-handled Colt revolvers the city marshal had strapped high on his waist. Buckskin shirt, cowhide vest, corduroy pants tucked inside his tall boots, and gal-leg spurs. looked like an Indian Chief in cowboy clothes. *Damndest dressed man I ever saw*, thought Eli Stagg.

Cherokee Tom knew practically everybody in Ardmore, but he didn't know the big ugly man sitting at one of the tables nursing a beer. He wasn't impressed by what the federal law was looking like these days. Cherokee Tom walked over and stood before the man's table.

"I'm the city marshal and I hear that you are a Federal man," said Cherokee Tom. "Why are you here?" Cherokee Tom's voice was as flat and hard as a billiard table.

"I come over from Ft. Smith, from Judge Parker's court. Supposed to meet a ranger coming up this way from Pecos, Texas. Supposed to take charge of two prisoners he is escortin'. Been waitin' three days. You ever hear of Pecos, Texas?"

"I have. But, why come here and not down there?"

"Hell, I don't know," growled the bounty hunter. "You understand how things work. You get orders to do this or that and you do them. You don't ask the reason behind it because there usually ain't none."

Cherokee Tom studied the graveled face of the federal man, saw the deputy's star he wore on his coat, the belted Colt revolver, the Creedmore leaning against the table.

"Don't believe I caught your name?" said Cherokee Tom.

The bounty man thought hard, thought hard as to the name on the papers he had lifted from the deputy's pocket. Damned if he could remember, never figured to be asked such a question. He saw the inquisitive stare of the breed lawman.

Failing to recall the murdered deputy's name from the legal papers, he said the only thing he could: "Stagg, Eli Stagg."

"Maybe I'll wire on to Pecos and see if there's a reason the party you're waiting on hasn't showed up yet."

" 'Tain't no use troubling yourself on such matters, marshal. I had just made up my mind to go on down the trail looking for them when you walked in. I'll be long gone time you hear back."

"Well, Deputy Stagg, it's a hard ride from here to Pecos, lots of dried up and empty land. Not at all friendly. Maybe you ought to stick around whilst I do some checking — could save you a peck of trouble?"

"Don't believe I will, marshal. Done waited long enough. Sooner I catch up with 'em, the sooner I can get back to Arkansas. You ever been to Arkansas?"

"No sir, I never have. But, I hear Judge Parker is a severe man?"

"Oh, that he is. You wouldn't want to commit an offense in Judge Parker's district." The conversation between the two men petered out. Each drew a breath, eyed the other, waited.

"Well, marshal, I guess there ain't no use sitting here jawboning, not when I got duties to perform . . ."

"Suit yourself," said Cherokee Tom. "You know your duties better'n me. I wish you luck." Cherokee Tom watched as the bulky man lifted himself from behind the table, gathered up his Creedmore, and walked on stumpy legs toward the door. The city marshal drifted to the lunch counter, ordered a slice of Dutch apple pie and black coffee, and when the cook laid the fare before him, Cherokee Tom said: "That man strikes me as false."

"What man?" asked the waiter.

But Cherokee Tom was already absorbed in his

211

pie and coffee and did not answer.

Caleb Drew was less than a day's ride right out of Ardmore. His thoughts had been on the man he was pursuing. His concern was over the fact that he had never been in a gunfight, never been under fire. Once the moment came, as it surely would come when he caught up to Eli Stagg, how would he act?

With some men, just wearing the badge was enough to bring them up short but not, Caleb surmised, a man who was mean and vicious enough to track down a deputy U.S. Marshal and murder him. A man like that would not be cowed by the sight of a badge.

Caleb Drew had never thought much about his own death. Selling barbed wire to ranchers was not a dangerous profession. Being a Federal Marshal was only dangerous politically, for the most part.

Now, for several days running, he had thought about death. And the thinking had put a knot in his guts and forced him to think of other things. But, in spite of the fear, he pushed on, feeling possessed, feeling he was without choices anymore.

The day was warm and pleasant, and he was growing accustomed to riding saddle horse and found himself enjoying it. The big steel-dust beneath him, the weight of the pistol on his hip, the bedroll tied behind the cantle, and the stock of the Winchester just behind his right leg — all gave him the sense of being a lawman. A true law-man.

He would be in Ardmore by first light of morning. If Eli Stagg was there, Caleb Drew told himself, the law would be prosecuted as well as he was capable of doing. Even if it meant someone dying.

Cherokee Tom sent a wire to the Texas Ranger station in Pecos. It read: *A man who calls himself Stagg and represents himself to be a Deputy U.S. Marshal from Judge Parker's court in Ft. Smith, Ark., has this day passed through here. He has stated to me, that he waited here for 3 days hoping for a rendezvous with one of your men and some prisoners. I believed this man to be an imposter from the first, but have no proof. He has now left this place stating that he is on the trail of his quarry. I consider my duty complete in this matter — Thomas Blue Feather, City Marshal, Ardmore, The Indian Nations.*

Cherokee Tom paid fifty cents to have the wire sent. It was a feeling he had about the man that had caused him to spend that much money to send a wire — an instinct — one that felt as strong as cheap whiskey. Life on the border was a mean and temporary thing, he reasoned. Might not hurt to let a fellow lawman know that there was trouble afoot — he'd expect the same if the tables were reversed.

Eli Stagg wasted no time in clearing the town. A man gets nosy, especially a lawman, there wasn't any telling what could come of a thing like that.

213

He was plum getting tired of waiting for the reward to come to him. He figured he'd just have to track it down. Tracking was something he was good at.

The first light of dawn lifted clear and cold over the shabby town of Ardmore. Cherokee Tom was already blowing steam off his second cup of coffee when the door rattled open.

"Are you the city marshal?"

"I am."

"My name is Caleb Drew, I'm a U.S. Marshal out of Ft. Smith. I'm looking for a man."

"Ardmore has had its share of Federal men from Ft. Smith lately," said Cherokee Tom.

"Tell me about the other one," said Caleb Drew.

"Was through here yesterday. Left yesterday. Did not seem to want to stay around once I asked him his business. Said he was on the search for a Texas Ranger and some prisoners. I didn't believe his story a whole hell of a lot, but he was wearing a badge, just like you."

"Did he give his name?"

"Said his name was Eli Stagg. Carried a big Creedmore. Could kill almost anything from a long ways off with a gun like that."

"Then I am on the right trail," said Caleb Drew.

"Would you like some of this coffee?"

"I would. Is there a place I can get some breakfast?"

"There is. I'll go with you so's we can talk."

They ordered eggs and fried ham, black beans and more coffee.

"How'd this fellow strike you?"

"As a man who didn't mind killing much. But anymore, this whole dang territory is filling up with such low life."

"Well, I plan on tracking him down. He murdered a deputy of mine."

"You'd best shoot him in the back if you get a chance, or anywhere else. A man like that, I would not trust nor give any opportunity to."

"How's the trail from here to Texas?"

"It's a good road, but bandits along the way. Camp off the road a good distance, and don't light too many fires, and you should be alright."

"Well, I had better be on my way," said Caleb Drew, draining the last of the coffee in his cup. "You have a fine little town here from what I see."

"It'll do, I suppose," said Cherokee Tom. "Not many places that'd hire a part Indian to run their law. That much I appreciate."

Caleb shook the lawman's hand and headed for the door of the restaurant.

"Marshal," said Cherokee Tom. "You be careful where you bed down at night. They've got snakes in Texas big as your leg."

Chapter Nineteen

They had walked for two full days without sighting a single living creature. The journey had been slow and arduous. Pete was weak from the loss of blood and the grievous wound, and they both suffered the lack of food. Their progress had been only half of what it should have been.

They had gathered mesquite beans and pounded them with rocks and ate them. They had also found some banana yucca and gathered and roasted the fruit from that plant. And they had been careful with the water. But they could not ignore the fact that Pete Winter's condition seemed to be deteriorating.

He had considered sending Katie on alone in hopes of finding a ranch. But he knew that without knowledge of the land, she would most likely become lost and perish. As for himself, he now held little hope that he would survive. He had had two straight nights of feverish dreams, dreams that saw him attending his own funeral.

He saw himself lying in a black casket wearing a black suit and white shirt and black cravat. He saw the casket being lifted into a glass-sided hearse that was pulled by four black horses through a town that he did not recognize. He saw the hearse climb a small barren hill where there was a graveyard. He saw a woman in a black dress crying, and when the wind lifted her veil, it was Katie

Swensen. Henry Dollar was there too, standing next to Katie Swensen. The older lawman's face was grim and full of sadness and he wore a dusty suit and held his battered old gray Stetson in one hand.

That's how the dreams went for two nights running.

He knew that somehow he had to save Katie. She did not deserve to die in the middle of nowhere, with no one to mourn her passing. She was too young for that.

He had tried several times to use his right arm, but without success. The bone had been shattered and if it healed at all, it would heal badly. He knew, and had known from the moment he had been struck by the Comanche's bullet, that he would never again be able to use the arm. He avoided thinking about it as much as was possible, but was not always able to ignore the fact that he was, and would be, crippled.

In spite of everything, Katie Swensen had not complained, nor shown any loss of resolve to find rescue. In addition to carrying her own weight, the canteen of water, and the extra pistol, she tended to him whenever they had rested, or bedded down for the night.

She had slept close to him, using her body as a way to keep him from becoming chilled. She had forgone some of her own drinking of the water in order to dampen his fevered forehead, and allow him extra to drink, knowing that he was in greater need.

They came to an arroyo and climbed down into it for the shade.

After several minutes of rest, he said: "Katie, I'm sorry that this has happened."

"Try not to talk, Pete. There's nothing you can say that will change our circumstances."

"That's true enough," he said. "But, if only I would have been a little more cautious, we might not be in this situation. I feel to blame and I want you to know that I am sorry."

"Sorry? Why should you be the one to feel sorry? It was my decision to have run off with Johnny Montana. It was my blindness that led me to stay with him through everything. I thought I was in love." She laughed at the notion.

"Pete, you just will never know how foolish someone can be when they think that they're in love. Pray that nothing like love ever comes your way."

She closed her eyes and remembered her papa, remembered how often he would make her wishes come true. It seemed to her now that she had always relied on men to make her happy.

She had relied first on her father. Later, it was the young suitors, boys really, who were willing to do anything for her, anything to make her happy. And then there was Johnny.

She had relied most on Johnny to make her happy. And now, as she lay in the only shade for miles and in the middle of nowhere, she realized that she had never been truly happy, and that her reliance on men had always left her wanting.

How strange, she thought, that she was now in the most desperate situation of her life, and a man was relying on her — not for his happiness, but for his survival.

She would save him, she promised herself. She would save him, or they would die together.

"Katie . . . are you alright?"

She opened her eyes.

"You were trembling," he said.

"I was just thinking about everything, about how strangely things turn out."

He came to her and placed his good arm around her shoulders.

"I know things look terrible bad, I won't lie to you about that. But, I think if we can last another day or two, we'll come up on something." They both knew that it was more brave talk than reality, but neither acknowledged it. Nonetheless, it felt good to her to have him hold her.

He felt her warmth and softness against him, as he had for the past few nights when she lay close to him. It was the greatest comfort to wake up and have her there, just as it was now to be holding her.

He felt the brush of her hair against his face. He lightly kissed her cheek. It seemed a natural matter to him, one that he could not resist any longer.

She turned her face to him. Her eyes searched his face. Her mouth was suddenly soft and sweet against his own. He had never had a woman kiss him before. He had kissed a few, but had never

219

had one kiss him. The comfort of it overwhelmed him. He kissed her back and she let him.

"Pete —" She rested her head against him and placed one hand on his chest. And for a long time, neither of them said anything.

"Seems funny," he said at last.

"What does?"

"Seems funny that with everything that's happened, that this would too."

"I wish that I had never met Johnny Montana," she said. "It should have been you that I met and fell in love with."

"Hush," he whispered. "There's no need for regretting something that has already happened. I guess we'd all change things in our lives if we could go back and do it over."

"I know. But, I made a damn fool of myself over that man and I don't know if I will ever forgive myself. He used me and I let him and I feel ashamed."

"I know you do, Katie. But the good Lord didn't make any perfect people — including me and you. We've got enough to face without facing the past."

She sat up and searched his face. "Pete, you can never know the kind of shame I feel about what I've done."

"That's where you are wrong, Kate. I know what it's like to feel shame, the kind you're talking about. I carry my own shame."

She stared at him with disbelieving eyes. "You are just trying to make me feel better about myself," she said.

"No, I'm not. What you did, you did because you thought you were in love and it was right to stick by the man you loved. I did something far worse, I helped hang an innocent man. And I did it because I was being high-minded."

She could see the pain in his face, the way his eyes looked off to somewhere.

"Why, Pete? Why would you do something like that?"

It was something that he had not spoken of but once since it had happened. It still haunted him.

"I was young and hot-tempered. I rode with a group of vigilantes before I joined the rangers. I thought we were doing the right thing — I always thought of myself as doing the right thing. It was a time and place when there were lots of horse thieves and cattle rustlers, and a big rancher named Wilkens blew hot air into my head about clearing the land of such trash.

"At that time, there wasn't any law to speak of, not in that part of the country. As it turned out, we caught a fellow we were sure was a cattle rustler. Wilkens gave the man a kangaroo court and then we hung him. We had caught him butchering a beef. Found out later from one of Wilken's line riders that the steer had died on its own and he had given the man permission to butcher it for his family — they were squatters. Nothing but starving squatters. The man had a wife and six children . . ." His voice trailed off.

"The worst of it was," he continued, "I never told what happened to the man that raised me and

221

gave me this job. I always felt too ashamed to talk about it. The only other person to know besides you is a man named Henry Dollar. He's a ranger too, but more like an older brother."

"I'm sorry that something like that happened to you," she said. She stroked his cheek and held him close.

"I'm sorry too, Katie. It is something I will always have to live with. It was Henry Dollar who taught me that a man's mistakes can just as easily cause him to become a better man as they can to destroy him. He was right."

"He sounds like a wise man."

"More than that, Katie, far more than that."

She kissed him again.

"What will become of us, Pete?"

"I don't know," he said. "But, I'm going to do everything in my power to see that you make it to safety."

She sighed and said, "Safety from this place will only mean going back to Arkansas and standing trial for my crimes. I am not so sure I want to be rescued, Pete."

He made a decision then and there, one that went against the grain of everything he believed in, everything he and sworn himself to.

"I won't let it happen, Katie. I won't let you go back to Arkansas."

"Pete, you can't make that decision. You're a lawman, don't break your trust for me."

It was at that moment that a miracle came churning out of a tunnel of dust.

They heard the thing before they could even see it. It was a rattling, clanging, banging apparition that seemed to rumble up out of the very earth itself.

"What is it, Pete?"

He hushed her so that they both could listen and watch above the embankment of the arroyo.

Through the shimmering waves of heat rising up off the floor of the prairie, the thing came lumbering into view. The nearer it drew, the louder it became. Finally, they could plainly see it to be a wagon. A wagon with a white canvas top.

"A pilgrim's wagon," said Pete.

Hanging from the wagon were an assortment of pots and pans glinting in the sun. They clanged and banged and rattled against one another with every jostling step taken by the team of mules that pulled the wagon.

A hundred yards distance, they could see that the team was being driven by a man — a woman sat by his side. Atop all the noise that the clanging pots and pans were making, the man was bellering a song — either that or he was cussing out his mules in a steady litany.

"Darndest looking salvation I have ever seen," said Pete, grinning at her.

The wagon came on, directly toward the arroyo. Pete and Katie struggled up the embankment and toward the oncoming contraption.

The driver of the wagon, a fellow whose beard was long and bushy enough to store supplies in, hauled back on the reins and brought the mules to a stiff-legged stop.

Next to the man was a dark-skinned woman as plump as a bullfrog. She had a moon face and narrow eyes. It was plain to see that she was Indian.

"Hullo and high hell!" called out the driver as he eyed them both. "Looks like you got yourself plum lost and busted up. A bad combination for these parts!"

Pete had been fully prepared to commandeer the wagon if need be.

"I'm a Texas Ranger on legal business," said Pete to the inquiring gaze of Bushy Beard. "We've run into some trouble a while back — renegade Comanches. We could use your help."

"Seems like you must have gotten the best of them!" shouted the teamster.

"How so?" asked Pete.

"Well, you ain't murdered!" Bushy Beard cut loose with a great laugh that exposed a wet hole of a mouth. When the spasm passed, he leveled a more serious look and said, "It does look like they got your horses, though. Them Comanch, the one thing they love almost as well as riding horses is eatin' them."

"No sir, they didn't get our horses," said Pete. "I shot them for breastworks."

"Well then, you denied them all the way around, good for you, son," said Bushy Beard handing the reins to the woman seated next to him before climbing down from the wagon.

"I'd say," he said, coming close to examine the

ranger's wounded shoulder, "that you're in need of some of Sister McKnight's medical care and maybe a swaller or two of her *Sorrowful Plains Elixir.* That's Sister McKnight, sitting up there in the wagon."

The woman's moon face remained stoic throughout the introduction.

"She's my wife, travelling companion, cook and confidant, and mother of several children, all of which have growed and turned wild and are scattered from here to the great ocean. She also makes the only curative known to revive man and beast alike and comes with a money back guarantee. She's part Apache and part Arapaho, but mostly Apache — too bad because it sometimes gives her more of a temper than is tolerable. But she's a good woman all around and knows most things I do, and a few I don't. Ain't that right darlin'?"

The stolid features of the woman gave way slightly to a coppery smile showing few teeth.

"My name is Billy Bear Killer, at least that is what *she* calls me," he said, jutting a thumb back over his shoulder toward Sister McKnight.

"My true name is Marion Brewster, but that ain't no sort of name for a plainsman, like I am. Especially so, if you are married to a woman that is part Apache and part Arapaho. You can just call me Billy."

Pete extended his good hand to the solid beefy grip of the teamster.

"I'm Pete Winter, this is Katie Swensen, and

225

we are glad as we can be to make your acquaint-ance."

"That shoulder of yours looks gruesome," said Billy Bear Killer, taking it upon himself to examine the wound. "I'd say it's best you climbed up in back of the wagon and have Sister McKnight prac-tice her medical abilities on it. You'll feel much better once she has."

The ranger looked down at Katie with eyes that fought off tears.

"Mister, I'd appreciate it if you could find some grub for Katie."

"Well sir, grub is just exactly what I had in mind. This looks like a good a spot as any to set down stakes for the night. Looks to be a purty sunset if those clouds stay off to the west like they are now. I'll prepare a fire, and soon's Sister's had a look at you, we'll put on the feedbag, and you can tell me more about them Comanches you run into."

Pete watched as Sister McKnight lowered her ample bulk down from the wagon and came and took him by the hand and led him to the back of the wagon. Wordlessly she motioned for him to climb in the back and lay down upon the quilts that were spread there.

Outside, he could hear Billy Bear Killer tell Katie: "Here's some lye soap and fresh water, I reckon you'll want to freshen up some for sup-per."

Then, he heard Billy Bear Killer begin his sing-ing once more as he undid the traces of the team of mules. The teamster's voice was like faraway thunder rolling out across the prairie.

It was as soothing as good liquor, as sweet as rain.

Chapter Twenty

Eli Stagg maintained a steady pace for three days running on his journey southward. He did not trust lawmen — injun, or otherwise — they were snoopy. As far as he was concerned, that half-breed lawman might have let his suspicions cause him to do some checking with Ft. Smith. If that was so, then it would be plain as a spinster's face that there wasn't any Eli Stagg held in the employ of the U.S. Marshal's office.

It was lonesome, ugly country, as far as the bounty hunter could see. The only spark of color was the bluebonnets that dotted the low rolling hills. The days turned hot and humid, and once he had to hole up because of a terrible downpour. And if that were not enough, his mount had turned up sore-legged to the point he had had to dismount and walk the animal for a day until he reached a small Mormon settlement and was able to buy a bottle of liniment to rub on the horse's foreleg.

Seemed like the farther away from the Ozarks he got, the more inhospitable the land became. It was not a place he would ever care to live, he told himself.

Caleb Drew was glad he had bought an extra mount in Ardmore. By changing horses every few hours, he always kept one of the mounts fresh and was able to maintain a good steady pursuit of his quarry.

The thought of turning back was never one he gave serious consideration to. Although, with each passing day, he had to admit to himself that he much missed his wife and children. But, what could he say to them, or to anyone else, if he came back empty-handed, knowing that he did not do his best. No, the pursuit had become something more than simply going after a killer, it had become personal.

He came to a small settlement and decided to ride in rather than go around.

A man wearing black clothes and a soiled white shirt came out to greet him.

"Welcome, friend," said the man in the black clothes. The man wore spectacles, a broad brimmed black hat and scuffed brogans. Caleb noticed that a number of community members hung back, stood in their doorways, or leaned over fences watching the encounter between him and the greeter.

"How do," replied Caleb. "I wonder if I might water my horses and buy a little grain for them?"

"You are welcome to water your animals, and we have some spare grain that we can give you. Food for yourself if you like."

Caleb Drew became aware that all the men were dressed similarly to the one he was talking to, as well as the boys, and that the women wore long black dresses and bonnets.

"We are Mormons," said the man in answer to

the unasked question that lay in the gaze of the lawman. "We never made it to brother Young's camp in Utah, not all do. We find this place to be one of good grass and fair weather and rich soil. A place of solitude and peacefulness as well. It will do for us."

"Thank you for the hospitality," said Caleb, dismounting and leading the two horses to a water trough. The man followed along behind, joined now by several other men and boys whose curiosity drew them out. The women and young girls remained near the houses.

Caleb noticed several fair-sized vegetable gardens, some sheep pens, corrals, out-buildings and some farming equipment — all neat as a pin.

He loosened the saddle on the mare he had been riding while she and the other horse drank at the trough.

"It looks like you all have made a nice place for yourselves here," said Caleb. "I don't reckon there are many Mormons in Texas," he commented further as a way of conversation.

"More than you might think," replied the man who then extended his hand. "I am Joseph Tinsdale, Elder. It is always good to have guests. You are welcome here." Caleb shook the hand, noted the strength in it.

"I'm Caleb Drew, Federal Marshal from Ft. Smith over in Arkansas." Caleb saw a flicker of caution pass through the elder's eyes.

"Not to worry, Mr. Tinsdale. I'm only passing through this way. I am in pursuit of a man who murdered a deputy of mine. I believe that he would have passed this way sometime in the last day or two."

The look of caution in Elder Tinsdale's gaze was replaced by one of recognition.

"A stranger did pass this way early yesterday morning. He purchased a bottle of liniment for his animal — sore legs, he mentioned. Not a friendly man. We offered him what we would any traveller: food, rest, water. But, he seemed not inclined to partake of our offerings."

"Tell me, Elder. Was this man big-chested with stumpy legs? Did he wear buckskins and carry a big bore rifle?"

"It does sound like the man, yes."

"Good, then I am gaining ground on him."

"You are welcome to stay for lunch," said Elder Tinsdale.

Just the mention of food renewed a forgotten hunger within the lawman. Trail grub was at best merely sustenance. Usually hardtack and salt pork and occasionally beans. He had given no time for the hunting of meat. None could be afforded in the pursuit of the killer.

Now, he weighed the desire to eat a good meal, with the need to continue the trail without let up. He decided that he could stand the nourishment and make up whatever small amount of time it might take to eat with these kind folks.

"I'd be obliged to sit down to lunch with you, Elder. I have not had a good meal since leaving Ardmore, three days ago. My missus is a good cook and I sorely miss the taste of well-prepared victuals." The decision seemed to please Elder Tinsdale for a broad smile creased his kindly face.

He was placed near the head of a long table that stood in the front yard of one of the main houses. All the men and boys removed their hats and sat with their heads bowed while a prayer was spoken by Elder Tinsdale. After which, the women and girls served them bowls of lamb stew, hot biscuits, fresh vegetables, and cold buttermilk.

It was as satisfying a fare as any he had ever eaten, and Caleb Drew found himself cherishing each bite. The men ate silently and with purpose, it seemed. Little or no conversation took place at the table. After all the men and boys had been served, the women and girls had taken places at a second table and ate in equal silence. Only the smallest children made any show — theirs, one of happy laughter.

Afterwards, they had invited him to dinner and to stay the night. He thanked them, shook several hands of the men and declined to stay longer.

"Elder Tinsdale," he said, as he prepared to mount. "You have a good community here. I wish you the best of luck for the future. I am willing to pay you for the meal, the water, and the grain you have given me for my horses."

"No need for payment, Mr. Drew. We cannot accept payment for the Lord's bounty. What we have was given to us by Him and we share it gladly. It is the Lord's way to help where we can. We will remember you in our evening prayers and wish you God speed in your journey. I hope that it does not end in violence."

"So do I, Elder, so do I."

He glanced back as he rode away from the small settlement, many of them waved their goodbys and he tipped his hat to them. He felt at once renewed by their kindness and refreshed by their generosity. And for once, his mind did not dwell on the task directly before him.

Eli Stagg had tracked both animals and men long enough to know when he himself was being trailed. There was nothing physical to indicate it, no sight or sound behind him to prove it. But, instinct told him that someone was on his trail. How far back, he could only guess. Who was tracking him was also just a guess.

Several times he had paused and waited, hoping that whoever it was on his trail would make the fatal mistake of being too close. But, no one came. Perhaps he was just being overly cautious he told himself, but then, it paid to be overly cautious and so the feeling would not leave him.

He had maintained such caution as well when passing others on the road, refraining from contact or casual conversation. He had no desire to be delayed or encountered. But, as the nagging suspicion grew that he was being trailed, he knew that he must stop long enough to lay an ambush for whoever it was behind him.

He maintained an eye for a place that would afford him hideout along the trail, a place where he could observe but not be seen. Unlike the wooded hills of Arkansas where ambushes could easily be laid, this Texas country seemed spare of any such opportunity.

He purposely slowed his pace in order to scout for spots from which to set an ambush in hopes that whoever it was behind him would catch up.

He eventually came to a broad but shallow looking river, the brown muddy flow broken only by the white riffles where it was most shallow. A small stand of cottonwoods lined the far shore. It would be the proper place for an ambush.

He touched heels to the horse, walking it into the river. The water rose only to his stirrups before receding again. He walked the horse onto the far muddy bank and in among the cottonwoods.

After hobbling the horse, he removed his saddle and gear, and placed them on the ground near the base of a good-sized cottonwood that afforded him both a clear view from whence he had just come and concealment.

He removed the Creedmore from the deerskin scabbard and laid its barrel to rest across the saddle. He judged the distance between his position and that of the far bank to be seventy yards, an easy shot for such a weapon.

He settled himself in a comfortable position, accommodating his wait with the taste of beef jerky and warm water from his canteen. A taste of good whiskey would settle just fine in a man's belly, he thought.

So would a lot of other things that two thousand

dollar reward money would bring: Whiskey, and women, and a new rifle. Some good horses maybe.

He checked the loads in his weapons, made sure his cartridges were dry by spreading them on a blanket in the sun. A man could never be too careful. Lots of men had died because their hammers fell on bad cartridges.

Caleb Drew had removed his jacket due to the heat of the day. He wore a fresh white linen shirt that he had packed as an extra and had put on the day before when eating lunch with the Mormons in their settlement.

His wife had bought him the shirt for his Federal appointment. It had come with a paper collar and paper cuffs, which he soon discarded. He wore crimson suspenders instead of a belt to hold up his denims. Strapped to his waist was the Peacemaker with a seven-and-one-half-inch barrel that he had paid fifteen dollars for. He had replaced the original walnut grips with ones of Mother of Pearl and then had the pistol nickel plated. It was a fine looking weapon. He had only fired it in target practice. It seemed a bit heavy, but he figured after all the expense, it would do.

Off in the distance he could see the bright green leaves of the cottonwoods fluttering in the wind. The horse had picked up the smell of water and had quickened its pace. He gave it its head, glad for the opportunity.

Eli Stagg saw the dust sign of a rider approaching from across the river. He set the rear sights that he had had especially mounted to the Creedmore. Resting the weapon across the seat of the saddle, he lay spread-eagled behind it.

The flat muddy river came into view as Caleb rounded a slight bend in the road. It was the color of creamed coffee.

Eli Stagg saw a single rider approaching the river from the far side. He drew a bead on the broadest part of the man — his chest.

As the rider came nearer the water, the bounty hunter could plainly see that it was not Cherokee Tom, as he suspected it might be all along. He was disappointed that it was not the lawman. He had sort of hoped it would be; the fellow was way too nosy, and too uppity to be wearing a badge and acting like a white man.

The fellow across the river looked as though he could be a drummer, except for the iron on his hip and the stock of a Winchester protruding from the saddleboot.

Caleb Drew had never even given it a thought that his badge remained pinned on the jacket he had removed earlier and tied to the back of his saddle.

The bounty hunter squinted to see if the rider across the river was wearing a star. He didn't see one. It would be an easy shot. He held his fire, though, waiting to see what the fellow was up to. A lawman had certain ways about him that other men did not. Lawmen were snoopy. He'd be able to tell by watching whether or not this fellow was snoopy.

Caleb Drew pulled up to the water, dismounted, and let his horses drink freely while he scanned the far shore. There were cottonwoods on the other side that he could catch some shade in and give the animals a chance to graze on sweet grass for a brief while. He was glad for the respite.

While he waited for the animals to finish drinking, he knelt to scoop some of the water into his hands and splash it over the back of his neck. As he did so, he noticed a fresh set of tracks leading into the river. He moved closer to examine them.

Eli Stagg saw the man inspecting the ground. *He surely ain't no drummer.* He drew the hammer back on the Creedmore.

In that instant, Caleb Drew recognized the possibility that the tracks could easily belong to his quarry. Perhaps, right now, the man was across the river laying in among the cottonwoods watching him — laying ambush for him.

Instinct caused him to reach for the Colt on his hip, the fingers touching the Mother of Pearl handgrips.

As they did, Eli Stagg squeezed the trigger of the Creedmore.

The boom of the big gun resounded among the cottonwoods, a large plume of smoke lifted itself from the hidden position. The thumb-sized chunk of lead smashed into the chest of Caleb Drew knocking him flat on his back. His horses broke and ran.

It was as though a great weight had fallen on him and held him pinned to the earth. A fire felt as though it were blazing in his chest and both his hands had gone numb.

Everything seemed to have suddenly slowed down, most of all his thoughts. He could feel the wet warm strain of blood spreading over his shirt front. He knew he had been shot. The realization frightened him. He was afraid to look at the wound, but he did so anyway. The white shirt was splattered a crimson that glistened in the sunlight.

He tried to move but found that he could not. The weight on his chest seemed to grow heavier. It was difficult to take a breath. He swallowed several times and felt the blood rising into his throat.

The sky above him was clear blue, as blue as he had ever seen it. He could hear something splashing in the river, could hear the splashing come nearer.

Eli Stagg waded into the water, his Creedmore reloaded and ready. He crossed cautiously, even though he knew that his shot had taken the stranger dead center — through the brisket. The man had not moved, except for a slight effort of his legs. But, old trapper's habits made the bounty hunter wary of the trapped.

The blood was beginning to cause him to choke and fight for breathing. He wished he had something to drink, something to wash the blood out of his throat. He could hear the sound of splashing growing closer and closer. *If only he could reach his pistol.*

Eli Stagg waded out of the river, his buckskins dark and greasy brown, and came to stand before the downed man. It was easy enough to see from the amount of blood soaked into the man's shirt front that the shot had been a mortal one.

"Who are you, mister?"

Caleb Drew felt the shadowy presence of someone, or something pass over him. He opened his eyes, saw the blurred features of a man, saw the man's mouth move, heard what sounded like echoes coming from the man's mouth.

"What — ?"

"I said, who the hell are you?" Eli Stagg bent at the waist and examined closer the drawn and twisted features of the wounded man. It was then that he finally came to recognize his tracker.

"I'll be damned to hell, you're that Federal Marshal back in Ft. Smith! The one that had everything handled. Haw! Looks like you done gone and got yerself kilt!"

The man's words were muted by the roaring inside Caleb Drew's head. He was feeling suddenly cold, as though he was laying in ice. He tried to understand what the man was telling him, trying to understand . . . and then he recognized the man!

"Please . . . ," he uttered. The word gurgled in the bloody throat. "Please . . . don't . . ." But, the words, the plea, seemed to die somewhere deep inside him.

The bounty hunter looked into the dying man's eyes. It was a look he had long grown accustomed to seeing in the eyes of animals he had trapped in the wilderness.

"You rode a long way just to get yourself kilt!"

He saw the bounty hunter step back away, saw the patch of sky above him once more, felt the warmth of sun strike his face, but still, his body was growing so very cold. He knew he was drowning in something he could not see but only feel.

He closed his eyes at the impending terror, prayed to a God that he had never taken the time to know, and then surrendered. Eli Stagg was already stripping away the lawman's possessions.

Chapter Twenty-one

After nearly six weeks, Carter Biggs found himself in the middle of nowhere, or so it seemed to him. All of his efforts had not brought him one step closer to his quarry, Johnny Montana.

Every day that passed drove home the realization that the quest for vengeance had been ill-fated. How he had ever hoped to track down the outlaw to begin with was beyond him now.

His journey had carried him through piney woods and rolling hills, through the bayous and swamps, beyond the forests and out into the open grasslands. Once he had crossed over into Texas, the country seemed to have gotten suddenly bigger and emptier than it ever had before.

The loneliness of the country had given him over to talking to himself. Without Lowell along to converse with, he felt a great longing to hear the sound of another human voice. His own would have to do.

"This is no place for a hog farmer," he admonished himself several times an hour, it seemed. "Nothing but yellow grass."

He had grown weary of the chase for more reasons than one. The fire in his belly to settle scores with the outlaw, Johnny Montana, no longer burned so hot.

"Forgive me old man," he prayed aloud as he rode over the vast open prairie, "but I just don't feel like I have the heart to keep going most days. It ain't that I don't want to do what is right by you, but I feel plumb lost in this Godforsaken country."

And then he would lapse into long spells of silence letting his bulk sway to the rhythm of the horse's step, listening to the whistle of wind against his sunburned ears. Sometimes he would cry.

He had ridden through rain and lightening storms, and once saw a tornado twisting in the distance. The sun and wind burned his neck and ears and turned his hands brown. And, it seemed, all day long he spat dust from his dry mouth.

Except for scattered herds of cattle, he saw no animal life other than a pair of pronghorn antelope that was too far away to shoot at — he shot anyway out of frustration.

He came to places where barbed wire fences made him change direction and once counted over two hundred coyotes that had been shot through the head and hung up by their tails on one of those fences — the smell was awful.

Compared to his beloved Autauga County, this land offered little compromise to man or beast. Even the plants were nothing more than survivors. Greasewood and prickly pear cactus, mesquite and yucca — thorny, sharp, inhospitable plants that seemed not much good other than for something to look at.

He missed the sweet grasses of his homeland, the bending willows, the towering oaks. He missed, too, the abundance of water. Texas water was precious; even the raindrops seemed to dry into dust the moment they hit the ground.

But it was more than trees and rivers and plants that was taking the heart out of Carter Biggs. It was more than missing the sound of rooting hogs and the smell of wood smoke and curing hams. It was more than the lonely journey that carried him farther and farther from home. What was weighing on the big man's shoulders more than anything was a desperately wounded brother left in the hands of a black-eyed Cajun swamp woman.

Carter Biggs was a man who prided himself in taking care of his own. It was a matter of honor.

But he had abandoned the boy in favor of some foolish vow he had clung to. That vow had not brought him any closer to Johnny Montana than it had the man in the moon.

It was stubbornness that had made him go on. He knew it. Stubbornness, like a pistol at his head, giving him no choice, pushing him on and on and on.

Poor ol' Lowell. Baby brother, Lowell. Probably lying dead under a mossy sod right now — chickens pecking on his grave.

He thought of the swamp woman, the Cajun. *Marie,* she called herself. Strange woman that both frightened and attracted him. *Hell, he had to leave.* Strange woman! *Stood right up to him, though. Stood up and talked him down.* Thinking of her made him anxious.

The town of Tascosa appeared through the haze of heat, a distant outline of low-lying buildings.

He had no idea what town it was, nor did he care. He was weary and sore and his mount was lathered, its head bent low to the ground.

Every board of lumber on every building was gray and weathered and curled, every nail head rusted. A few tents, a few buildings — that was Tascosa, he saw the name on several of the buildings painted in dull black letters a long time ago.

BEER & WHISKEY was one of the faded scripts above a narrow little shebang that seemed near ready to collapse inwardly upon itself. It would do, he told himself as he turned the animal's head in toward the hitch rail.

He didn't bother slapping the dust from his person, and out of habit, he looked around to see if Johnny Montana was among any of the patrons — he wasn't, nor did Carter Biggs expect him to be. It didn't seem to matter as much as it had in the last town, nor the town before that.

He ordered a whiskey and a beer chaser and the bardog announced that such purchase earned him the right to the free lunch that set at the end of the bar.

Flies circled and landed on the stacks of sliced beef, bread and pickles. Stalks of celery stood in a glass of water. He brushed away the flies and made a sandwich, then a second and found a table at which to sit where he did not feel so crowded by others.

The bartender brought over another glass of beer and without protest, Carter paid him a nickel for it.

As he ate, he noticed several men coming and going through the rear door of the place, heard some commotion, paid it idle curiosity.

A man stopped briefly at his table, leaned on it with both hands and with a twist of his mouth asked: "Hey there, stranger, are you gettin' in on the dog fight out back? It is about to start and they are laying bets now." Carter gave him the eye until he moved on.

In the next few moments, the entire population of the bar headed out the back door. His curiosity got the better of him.

Picking up a sandwich in one hand and a glass of beer in the other, he walked toward the back of the building and stepped outside.

A crowd had gathered in a circle. They were all men and excited. He worked his way into a position to be able to observe exactly what was taking place.

Heavy wagering was going on. Men with paper money in their fists hooted and yelled to place down their bets.

Across the far part of the circle, Carter saw a red-bearded man holding the leash on a stout gray bull terrier. Nearer to where he stood eating the sandwich, Carter saw a slightly built man, who wore a derby, pencil-thin moustache and nice looking suit of clothes. The man was holding the collar of a shaggy black animal that more nearly resembled a wolf than a dog.

"Come'n Coorigan," shouted the dandy across the ring to the red-bearded man with the gray

245

bull. "You surely don't believe that little pup of yours will be much more than a good meal for Sampson here, der ya?" The dandy flashed a smile that lifted the ends of his thin moustache.

Red Beard gritted his reply though the bush of beard that flowed nearly to his belt buckle.

"That black bastard of yours won't know what hit him once't Buck's jaws get locked down on his throat! And maybe when he's done with that mangy critter of yours, I'll let him have a taste of you as well!"

The crowd roared with delight over the open hostility that flowed between the two dog handlers.

"All bets in!" shouted a man carrying two fistfuls of money and clutching a ledger hook under his arm.

"Let 'em rip!" he ordered the dog handlers.

The gray terrier shot across the pit on short muscled legs almost before the dandy had loosed the shaggy black. The snarl and growl of each animal ripped the air, the black's lips curled back over the large canine teeth.

The bull barely missed black's throat as the black twisted sideways just in time to miss the fatal bite. Each cur raised itself on hind legs and lunged at the other. The bull was lightening fast and relentless. The black drew first blood just behind the bull's head, but it only seemed to inflame the attack of the smaller dog.

The bull caught the exposed flank of the black and its jaws snapped shut causing the black to yelp and howl. The hound's anguish drew a chorus of shouts and curses from some, laughter from others.

Somehow, the black managed to spin away from the snapping jaws of the terrier and began to inflict its own damage by raking its fangs across the rock-like head of the bull, tearing part of one ear off, leaving it a bloody flap.

The two fighting beasts worked their way back and forth across the man-made ring, each trying to secure a death hold on the other. Flecks of foam and blood dripped from their jaws and splattered in the dirt and on the toes of the men's boots.

The slashing fangs of the black scored a sudden but brief victory as they blinded one eye of the terrier — the only point at which the bull seemed hurt and gave ground.

Each draw of blood, each new wound, excited the crowd and men whistled and hooted and stomped their feet.

For all its size and power, however, the black was losing ground to the muscled fury of the bull. The fatal mistake came when the terrier rolled the black up, causing the animal to loose its feet and fall over onto its back.

The bull's fangs closed suddenly and solidly on the black's throat, the sharp fangs buried themselves deeply, and the mighty jaws clamped shut with such brutal force that the black's throat was crushed.

A desperate flurry of hind legs, and then the black went limp. The bull shook its head furiously swinging the body of the black as though it were a rag doll.

A mixture of groans and cheers rose from the spectators.

"Call him off, God damn it!" shouted the dandy, the handler of the black. "Call him off now, or I'll blow his bastard head off!" A small pistol, a nickel-plated pocket gun, flashed sunlight in his hand.

Red Beard looked across the ring at the dandy, the broad grin of satisfaction leaving his face as his eyes dropped to the small pistol in the dandy's fist.

"You shoot my dog you little priss, I'll bust your head open with a board."

"I mean it," shouted the dandy. "It's over — you've won your bet, now call him off!"

"When he's done, is when I'll call him off!"

Carter saw the dandy step forward, step into the ring and fire the pistol into the bull's head. Five shots, like the pop of firecrackers filled the air. The dog flopped over on its side, the black still locked in its jaws.

"You darty son of a bitch!" The Irishman's face burned red with anger, his fists balled into meaty knots as he charged from the crowd, charged across the earthen ring toward the dandy.

The dandy raised the shiny pistol, held it at arm's length, and without so much as a waver or a flinch. pulled the trigger, and his sixth and final shot drilled a neat hole into the center of Red Beard's forehead. The man fell face forward into the dust, fell as though pole-axed.

"I asked him to do the right thing," said the

248

dandy. "Asked him to call off his hound." The crowd had fallen as silent as novitiates on Sunday morning.

"He had his chance, damn him. You all saw that!" Several heads nodded in mute agreement.

The dandy stood, feet apart, his derby cocked slightly over his forehead, his jaw jutted forth, stood as though he was expecting a challenge from someone in the crowd, a friend of the dead man's, perhaps. But no one stepped forward.

"Well then, it looks as though I'm the winner after all. That being the case, then the drinks are on Ian McDuff," he said, jabbing a thumb into his chest. "And may the Scots always prove the Irish are nothin' more than durty little potato farmers."

It was a high insult, but if there were any other Irish in the crowd, none took offense at the remark as everyone filed back inside the tavern on the heels of the Scot, who waved a fistfull of dollars in one hand and the spent nickel revolver in the other.

Carter Biggs found himself standing alone, staring at the bodies of the dead man and the two fighting dogs. It was a pitiful callous sight on which to rest his gaze.

It was what Texas and the frontier had come to represent to him: sudden violence, death, uncertainty.

He stood for a long time staring at the bodies before turning away. He had decided. He would return to learn the fate of his brother, Lowell. His quest for Johnny Montana was over. He no longer had the heart for it.

He took off the pistol he wore and stuffed it in his saddlebags and then he found a livery, sold his horse and saddle and found the train station. He purchased a ticket east with connections through to New Orleans. And when he finished paying the teller, he went outside and sat on the platform and smoked a cigarette and waited for his train to come.

Never again would he return to Texas, and never would he know just how close he had come. Johnny Montana was riding a buckskin horse less than one hundred miles from where he sat and waited for the Lone Star Flyer.

Chapter Twenty-two

Johnny Montana rode the mare hard, too hard. After several miles, the animal began to falter. Reluctantly, the outlaw slowed his pace. He estimated that he had maybe eighty miles in all to cover in returning to the spot where they had been attacked by the Comanches.

It had been four days since he had ridden away from the buffalo wallow, maybe five, he wasn't sure — hadn't kept accurate count. He wanted to find them. He wanted to find them more that anything in the world. He wanted back what was his.

He rode in anger, seething anger. The anger that had been building in him ever since the ranger had "shown him up" in front of Katie. But, she was part of it too, he reasoned. She had fawned and played coy around the kid lawman. She had turned her loyalties, had sided with the ranger over him.

They had stepped all over his pride, the two of them. He wasn't going to just let a thing like that go. The reasons for going back, for seeking revenge kept snapping through his mind like banners in a wind.

It would be an easy enough task once he caught up with them. He'd dust the lawman in front of her, and then he'd take from her what he had been missing a long time, and after that . . . well, he wasn't sure exactly what he would do after that.

The thought of her and the lawman together galled him. He was anxious to use the gun on the ranger. No matter how he killed the kid, it somehow wouldn't seem enough the way he thought about it. It could never be enough for the humiliation he had suffered.

The dusky rose sky of evening lay before him. He'd have to make camp soon — one more night on this godforsaken prairie in this godforsaken Texas. Texas had proved to be the worst decision he had ever made in his life. Once he settled score with Katie and the ranger, he'd leave for sure, he told himself. *Maybe California.* He heard things were good in California. He'd heard a fellow couldn't go wrong in California.

Henry Dollar felt the gripping ache of broken ribs and the pounding pain of his swollen face with every step the animal beneath him took. Still, he kept the horse at a steady and deliberate pace.

He had swallowed some of the laudanum and after twenty minutes, it began to take effect. It was like the physician that had given it to him said: It took the edge off the pain, but made everything suddenly seem slow and lazy, and he found himself having to hold onto the saddle horn with both hands.

Ahead of him somewhere rode the outlaw.

The wagon of Billy Bear Killer and Sister McKnight rolled to a halt near the banks of a wide river that flowed smooth and brown.

"Well, here we are, children," announced Billy in a happy voice. Sister McKnight sat at her usual place on the wagon seat next to Billy. Pete and Katie rode in the back, protected from the sun by the canvas cover stretched over the iron ribs like old skin.

The pair climbed out of the wagon to a late afternoon sky that glowed copper. The jolt of the wagon had been harsh and uncomfortable, but not nearly as much as was being afoot in such country.

"What's she called?" asked Pete, pointing to the river.

"Don't reckon I know her proper name," said Billy Bear Killer. "I call her the Big Muddy. I've seen her swoll up so big she's carried dead cattle, trees, wagons, and boulders down through her. When it sometimes rains a lot early part of the year, she can be fiercesome. Right now, she's near as peaceful as a baby. Except for the quicksands in her bottom."

Billy had a chaw of tobacco in his cheek and a bottle of Sister McKnight's elixir in his back pocket, which he pulled out and offered to Pete with a cautious glance at Katie.

"Jus' medicine, ma'am," he assured.

Pete declined. "I'm feeling better, Billy."

"Suit yerself, youngster," said the squaw man, tipping the bottle up to his lips. And after a long hard swallow that saw Billy's Adam's apple bob up and down like a cork in water, he wiped his lips and said, "Preventative medicine, the best kind."

Billy set about taking care of the mules while Sister prepared a fire, took down several of her pots and pans hanging off the wagon, and began preparations for the evening meal. Katie offered to help, but Sister only acted like she didn't understand.

"She's kinda fussy about her kitchen," explained Billy. "Indian's got certain ways about 'em. Sometimes even I don't understand. Best to just stand back and let her do it. Why I remember once I had this ol' dog and he come up missing one day. Times was hard for me and Sister back then. I still think that maybe Sister cooked up that dog of mine in her pot. I don't know to this day whether or not I ate my own dog. I never did have the spunk to ask Sister about it." Katie swallowed hard over the story, unsure as to whether Billy was fooling her.

Pete offered to help with the mules and Billy gave a toothy grin.

"Me, I ain't so particular when it comes to getting help with the work. Take them traces off that far one, but watch his rear 'cause he'll sure kick the bejezzus outta you if he gets the chance."

Billy allowed Pete to help him water the mules before putting on their hobbles. Then, taking his double barreled shotgun, he walked upstream and disappeared. Half an hour later, Pete heard the boom of the gun go off, and a half hour after that,

Billy walked into camp carrying a pair of sage hens.

"Sister loves these," he said, holding the birds up in the air. "I love 'em too. Sister has a special way when it comes to cooking birds."

Later, they ate. It was true. Sister did have a special way with cooking birds. Pete and Katie both paid their compliments to Sister for the delicious fare. Sister lowered her eyes at such comments, but it was plain to see that she enjoyed their attention over her.

"It sure seems like you and Sister have a good life," said Pete. "Although I would find it hard to survive in such a place as this."

"Well, me an' Sister don't mind, and it ain't as harsh and desperate as it seems at first glance. Fer one thing, Sister could cook a bush and it'd make yer mouth water. And me and this old scattergun can shoot purty straight when it comes to putting game in the pot. Once every while, an antelope or a muley pays us a visit, that's when Sister really shines." Billy grinned and spat into the fire.

"As far as the rest," continued Billy. "Whenever me and Sister hit us a town, we sell her *Sorrowful Plains Elixir*. Folks have come to expect us. They pay a dollar a bottle and swear it cures their rhemuatiz, flux, dropsy, and memory. One old feller told me it even cured his plumbin . . ." Billy remembered the presence of Katie and said, "Sorry ma'am, I did not mean to offend."

"It's all right, Billy, no offence taken."

"What's in Sister's Elixir that makes it work

255

on so many ailments?" asked Pete, genuinely curious, for the liquid had seemed to have had somewhat of a curative effect on the pain in his shoulder.

"Can't say," answered Billy. "Sister keeps her recipe a secret, even from me. Which is alright, because maybe if I knew what she put in it, I wouldn't drink it." Billy's laugh wheezed like a bad bellows and he took a swallow of the Sister's elixir to his own delight.

"How far are we from the nearest town?" asked Pete, staring off at the brown river.

"That'd be Mormon Springs — 'bout forty some odd miles."

"I need you to take us there, Billy."

"Sure, me and Sister was headed that way anyhow. We're running low on sugar. I get grumpy when I don't have sugar in my coffee."

"I'll see that you get reimbursed for your trouble, Billy."

"Well consider it done," said Billy. "I reckon I better fix you up a night shelter a'fore it gets dark."

Pete offered to help, but Billy said he could do it easy. Billy made a lean-to out of a tarp and some branches he hacked from one of the cottonwoods lining the river's edge. Then, he spread a pair of bedrolls and announced it home for Pete and Katie. Each looked at the other, but made no comment.

Billy helped Sister McKnight take the cooking pots and tin plates down to the river to wash them, scrubbing them with sand and the muddy brown water. The whole while, Katie and Pete could hear the couple conversing in a language that was unfamiliar. Once, Sister McKnight laughed and jabbered and waved her finger at Billy and then he laughed too.

They returned from the river, each laughing, carrying their pots and plates.

As a way of answering the curious look of their guests, Billy said: "Sister's in a right good mood. Seems you two eating all of her cooking has made her happy as giggle juice. Sister says she's wanting that we should go into the wagon now and do a bit of talkin'. Anytime Sister's in that good of a mood, I best be taking advantage of it. I ain't getting any younger!" Billy laughed uproariously and squeezed an arm around Sister. Her dark moon bunched into a smile.

"See you two in the morning," said Billy.

Later, when she and Pete sat under the lean-to, Katie said, "They are like happy children."

"Good people," said Pete. "They seem to know something about living the rest of us are missing."

The sky had turned from copper to rose to purple. A full moon perched itself on the horizon for a time, and then slowly lifted in the sky.

Pete could not help but notice how beautiful Katie looked in the moon's light.

"Billy really seems to love her, doesn't he?" said Katie.

"He admires her like gold and silver," said Pete.

"It would be nice to have something like that."

"You mean to be like they are together?" he asked.

"Yes."

"Katie, I think it could be that way with us, if we wanted it to be."

She turned to look at him, her eyes searching his face, looking into his gaze.

"I wish it were so."

"I can understand how Billy must love Sister," said Pete. "I can understand that now . . . now that I know you."

She sighed, placed a finger to his lips.

"Don't say such things, Pete. I will only want to believe them."

"What is wrong with that?"

"You forget that I am a criminal, but I don't forget that."

"I don't care about that," he said.

"You should, Pete, you should."

"It doesn't matter anymore, Katie. As far as I am concerned it doesn't matter anymore."

"It does to me."

"Katie, I think I am in love with you."

"I know."

"Well?"

"What do you want me to say, Pete? That I love you too? What difference will it make?"

"A lot to me."

"Pete, don't love me. Find someone else to love, someone you can have a life with."

"I can have a life with you, Katie. I want to have a life with you."

She moved against him, took his face in her hands.

"Do you, Pete. Do you really?"

"Yes, more than anything."

"What if . . . when we get to Arkansas . . . what if . . ."

"Hush," he said. "We're not going to Arkansas. As far as I'm concerned you are innocent of the charges against you. As far as I'm concerned, it is Johnny Montana that is wanted. No one's going to know who you are, no one will even suspect."

"But what about you?" she asked. "What about your job as a lawman?"

His laugh was without humor.

"Who ever heard of a one-armed lawman," he said. "This shoulder will never heal so's I can use my arm. I'm finished as a lawman, Kate." She could see, in his sad eyes, that his shoulder was not the only thing wounded.

"Besides," he said, putting his arm around her, "there's other things in life than being a lawman. It doesn't matter if you'll be with me."

"I will, Pete. I promise you I will."

"You won't mind the fact that I'll be crippled in this arm?"

"Why should I," she said with a smile. "Between us, we have three good arms." He found himself laughing for the first time since before their journey had begun.

"I guess we do at that," he said.

Chapter Twenty-three

The trail from Mormon Springs proved to be of good grass. The dun had a smooth gait and the battered lawman was grateful for that.

He had picked up a fresh trail early and stuck with it. The way the sign read, the horse was moving at a gallop, moving hard. A man that rode his horse that way and for that long was in a hurry. He was looking for a man in a hurry.

The trail left by the outlaw may have been easy to follow, but the ride itself proved difficult. The ranger's jaw throbbed with sharp pain, the eye and cheekbone above it were painfully swollen, and the broken ribs seemed to be like knives being thrust into his side.

The troubling thing about his injuries was that the eye that was swollen closed was his primary eye, the one he used for shooting. If it came to fast gunplay, he would have to rely on instinct — a consideration he found little comfort in.

Several times, he coughed up blood. But it was old blood and so did not concern him as much as it might have.

Even though he had the pain killer, laudanum, in his saddle bags, he allowed his pain to become insufferable before reaching for the blue bottle. And even then, he was considerably careful about the amount of the liquid he drank.

But come the night, when the chill set in, increasing his pain, he relied on the laudanum to bring his ease. The first night, however, brought on terrible nightmares that caused him to come awake in a sweat.

Then, too, there was the fact that he was unable to chew any food and was only barely able to take in water from his canteen in sips. The lack of nourishment further weakened him. He was a big man, a man that needed the fuel of a full meal.

By the second day, he wasn't sure if it was the laudanum, the lack of grub, or the injuries that caused him to feel so light-headed.

Twice that day he thought he saw towns off in the distance, only to have them disappear, and once he nearly fell from the saddle, coming to just in time to get a grip and pull himself upright.

He heard strange noises, and possibly voices, that could have only come from within his head.

On the evening of the second day, he had come upon a trickle of a stream, barely enough for the horse to lower its muzzle and drink from. A lone cottonwood stood sentinel, some of its upper branches burned black from an old lightening strike.

He eased himself down, and without attempting to unsaddle the dun, sat with his back against the tree. It was an hour until dark, but he could not go on any longer.

Tying the reins of the animal around his wrist, he took a sip from the blue bottle and closed his eyes.

Sleep came quick.

His eyes suddenly opened. A man was standing over him, a pistol in each hand.

The man had a face that was familiar.

The man lifted the pistols and pointed them downward. He tried reaching for his own revolver, but it was not there. The man laughed and thumbed back the hammers of his pieces.

"Come to kill you, you bastard!"

The blasts from the pistols jarred him from his sleep. His heart beat hard against his chest, it felt as though he was drowning.

The night was black, the air cool, no moonlight, only the soft trickle of water and the dun cropping grass with slight tugs of the reins tied around his wrist.

He took several deep breaths, trying hard to shake the sluggish effects of the laudanum and the nightmare.

The blue bottle was still in his hand, he looked at it and flung it away, heard it shatter against something. "To hell with this," he muttered aloud. "I'm not putting anymore of this misery into me."

He eased himself onto his belly and scooped handfuls of the creek water up to his mouth and splashed it over his neck, loosed his kerchief and wetted it and held it against his jaw until he was fully alert.

He leaned back against the tree and closed his eyes to the pain.

He thought about Pete. Pete had been like a kid brother to him. Pete had been like Captain Ben's own son. It would be hard to have to tell the Captain that Pete was dead, hard to have to bury the boy, just like it had been to bury Jim McKinnon.

A man shouldn't have to die so early in life, he thought grimly.

Carefully, he took his makin's and rolled a shuck, struck a match to it and inhaled deeply. The hot warm smoke of the cigarette seemed to soothe his jaw and quiet his nerves.

Damndest time of my life, he told himself.

He sat and listened to the night; small frogs croaked from somewhere near by like they were protesting one another's presence and his presence.

The isolation of the moment caused him to examine himself, his past, his future.

After nearly forty years of living, his life was down to a single room in a Pecos boarding house, one saddle, one horse, two pairs of boots, a few clothes, a savings account of not more than two hundred dollars, and a dozen or so folks he could call friends. It didn't seem like a lot for a lifetime of living.

His thoughts turned to Josepeth Miller. Josie. He wondered how she had received the news of her husband's death — death delivered by his own hand. How would a thing like that set with her?

She had been the one true surprise in his life. He remembered how she had struck him the day he rode up to her house and saw her standing there, a plain unhandsome woman. Her plainness had proved her true beauty and she had captured his heart.

263

"Josie," he mumbled through swollen lips. He wished he were with her now. Not because of the pain or the isolation, but simply because he missed being with her.

His days of cantinas and dancing señoritas were in the past. He thought of Josie and yearned for a home, a place to elevate his feet and sit in front of a warm fire and talk about the day. A place where he could get up in the morning and not have to ride out after some desperado and sleep on the ground and eat trail grub.

Sitting there with the fire in his jaw and the ache in his ribs, such dreams seemed a long ways off.

Practically all his life, he had lived alone, worked alone, and stayed alone. Up until now, it had not been a life he minded. But each thought of Josie and what could be was changing that.

There was one other thing that he thought about as he stared up at the black night, at the distant stars, and wondered what all men, sooner or later, wonder about: his own mortality.

In some ways it seemed as though he had already lived a long time. But, there were other times when it seemed as though he had only begun to get the hang of living. It sort of seemed like that ever since he had met Josie.

The cigarette burned down between his fingers and he stubbed it out.

The only future he could see for himself right now was to track down the man ahead of him, to find Pete.

He regained enough strength in the resting to be able to unsaddle the dun and put on its hobbles. Finding his place once more against the tree, he pulled the horse blanket up around his shoulders and soon fell into a peaceful, exhausted sleep.

Morning found him sore but rested. He touched lightly at the jaw, noticed the swelling seemed to have gone down and was able to see a bit more out of the eye. A careful check of his ribs found them still sore, but tolerable.

He searched through his saddlebags and found a piece of beef jerky, broke off a bit and slipped it into his mouth. Chewing was painful, nearly impossible, but he worked the jerky slowly between his teeth as best he could and gained the flavor from it.

He walked the dun into the depression of the stream in order to lower the height of raising the saddle onto its back. He had to rest before cinching up. Finally, with one mighty effort, he stepped into the stirrup and swung into the saddle.

He touched spurs to the animal and walked it out of the creek.

Once more, he picked up the trail of the galloping horse.

Chapter Twenty-four

They had been camped for three days along the river Billy Bear Killer called the Big Muddy. The grass was rich and sweet for the animals — Billy said they needed the rest and graze and that soon they'd be as fat and happy as Indian babies. The whole while the weather had been warm and soothing.

Pete Winter had, at first, been anxious to go to Mormon Springs, but so pleasant had been their delay along the river with its good grasses, warm sun, and good company, that he found himself enjoying the respite.

Sister McKnight had twice daily attended to his wound, putting fresh bandages on with a salve she dipped from a tin that smelled godawful, but seemed to have gone a long way in healing the injury. She also spoke words over him — Apache or Arapaho, he was not certain. She also made him take a tablespoon of *Sorrowful Plains Elixir* six times a day. He wasn't sure if *that* did him any good, but it seemed to please her to no end.

Billy Bear Killer spent his time hunting birds, mending harnesses and greasing the wheels of the wagon. When he wasn't doing those things, he sat in the shade and twanged a Jew's harp and tapped his toe.

The rest had done Katie Swensen good as well. Pete noticed how color had returned to her cheeks, and how she had a tendency to smile and stay close to him. Sometimes, thinking about his crippling wound, he would feel blue. When he did, she would notice and tell him that Billy Bear Killer would throw him in the river if he did not cheer up immediately. It usually brought a smile back to his face.

At times, they whiled away the hours, sitting under the shade of the lean-to, talking, watching the river's flow, listening to the sounds of songbirds that flew down to the river to drink and splash at its edges.

"My arm is useless," he would sometimes tell her.

"That don't mean a thing to me, Pete Winter," she would say.

"What good is a one-armed man?" he would say when he was feeling especially blue.

"Pete Winter," she would tell him. "I don't care if you don't have any arms, that is not what makes you a man, not in my book. And that is not why I have come to feel about you the way I do. Now, if you do not hush such talk, *I'll* throw you in the river myself!" And then he would apologize to her for his blue mood and they would go for a walk along the river holding hands and he would feel much better.

They were sitting around the fire when Billy approached after having had a long and chatty conversation with Sister McKnight.

"Sister is curious about the redness of your hair, Miss Swensen. She wants to know how you came by it. I tried my best to explain to her that some white folks has got red hair, but it's a hard thing for her to understand — especially since Indians only have black hair. She said she surely would admire having red hair like yours. She's much impressed."

"Tell Sister that all the women in my family have red hair, Billy. Tell her that if she would like, I'll cut her a lock of it." Billy smiled broadly, turned and spoke to Sister. She held out her hand.

"Seems you have made a friend for life, Miss Swensen. She'd admire the gift."

"You mean right this moment?"

"I believe so — Indians have a way of taking everything to mean right now." He handed her a knife with a bone handle.

"It don't have to be much," he said. "Be careful of that blade little sister, it's as sharp as a nagging woman's tongue."

Katie found a good strand in the back of her head, something she figured would not show so much, but yet be enough to satisfy Sister McKnight.

She handed the hair to Billy who in turn handed it to Sister. Sister seemed pleased and so did Billy. He jumped and clicked his heels.

"Waugh, I don't know if anyone can stand it or not, but the last time me and Sister was up to Mobeetie, I swapped me a pair of Mexican spurs for a fiddle!" He clapped his hands and rubbed them together.

"I'd say it's time for a jamboree. I ain't never

played anything but my Jew's harp, but I'm willing to give that old fiddle a saw and see what comes out. Katie and Sister can bang pans, and Pete, you can stomp your feet!"

Billy went to the wagon and dug around beneath the blankets and supplies and pulled out a black leather case. He produced a scarred fiddle and a bow with several strands of hair hanging from it.

"I don't suppose you know much except chasing down bad men," shouted Billy. "But maybe you could get them gals up and dancin' while I play us a tune."

Pete felt a flush of embarrassment.

"Naw, Billy, I'm not much of a dancer."

"Well now son, these gals is goin' to be mighty disappointed unless you can figure out how to play with one good arm and let me do the dancin'. We can't have us a dance without music!"

"Come on, Pete," urged Katie, reaching for him. "It doesn't have to be anything fancy — let's just you and me and Sister step to the music."

With a degree of reluctance he gave in to their call. Billy put the bow to the fiddle and scraped once down and once back.

"Lord almighty!" he yeowed. "That sounds like someone skinnin' cats — give me a minute to figger this dang thing out." Billy worked the bow back and forth across the strings, twisted the tuning pegs a little and then, magically, he began a lively reel.

"That's a darn miracle!" shouted Pete.

"I was only fibbing," grinned Billy, "when I

said I never played one of these. I used to play in a professional band that even had a tuba in it. Now come on and let's get to dancin'."

Pete and Katie and Sister McKnight hopped and danced in a circle around the fire. Katie, holding hands with Pete and Sister, demonstrated a few steps they could do. And, at one point, Billy got so caught up in the fun, he laid the fiddle down and joined them, singing out a tune in a rich deep voice that surprised them all.

"I was a singer, too," he laughed.

Once started, Billy was reluctant to let them rest. They wore a path dancing around the fire. Even Pete had to admit that it seemed great fun. For the first time since he had been shot, he had forgotten about his wound. Dancing in the firelight, Katie holding his hand, Billy and Sister's laughter, Peter Winter realized how happy he was to be with them, to be with Katie. He knew that he loved her and would do anything to preserve that love.

Johnny Montana saw the distant glow of fire-light, heard the sounds of fiddle music and laughter. He rode the blaze-faced mare up on a slight rise of land until he could more clearly see the camp fire and the people dancing around it.

It was too dark to make out who the celebrants were, but he could see the fire's light reflected in the river that ran between him and the campers.

He dismounted and squatted on his heels watching and listening to them. And then he recognized a woman's voice, a woman's laugh and his heart quickened. It was Katie's voice. Her voice came well across the water, across the night. That it was her voice, he could not be mistaken.

He cursed silently. There was only one man she could be having fun dancing with — the Texas Ranger!

His urge was to go over and shoot up the camp, to take back what was his. But as smooth as the river flowed, he could not bring himself to cross it, not at night he couldn't. The old fear of drowning, the dreams he had about it, left him fearful of doing such a thing. He would wait until daylight, and then search for a safe place to cross, take the camp by surprise at first light. The plan eased his mind.

"Go ahead little woman. Go ahead and have your fun tonight. Tomorrow, I'll come and get you and you won't be so happy and your ranger won't be so happy neither."

Pete finally waved a hand in the air at Billy who was sawing a lively jig on the fiddle that sounded like demons were trying to escape the strings.

"I have to stop," he said with exhausted laughter. "I'm plum wore out, Billy! This dancing business is a whole lot more work than it looks."

Billy grinned, but finished the tune with a nice flourish and held the little instrument high in the air.

"You are a plum toe tapper, Pete," he said, bowing at the waist. "My, but you have worked both

Miss Katie and Sister into a glisten, look how rosy their cheeks glow."

Katie leaned against Pete, her arm around his waist.

"You were terrific," she said and kissed him. He flushed embarrassed at the public display, but Sister and Billy clapped their hands and hooted.

When Billy saw the young man's deep blush, he said, "I guess it *is* getting late. Me and Sister ought to be bedding down. Come morning, we head into Mormon Springs and drop you two off. You can catch the stage line out of there for just about anyplace you'd care to go."

The announcement brought with it a certain sad finality.

Katie had especially grown fond of Billy and Sister, but more, she had cherished these last few days of them all being together like children at play. Her and Pete, Billy and Sister. It was like an adventure of the heart, and one that she knew now was ending.

She had nearly, in those few happy hours, forgotten about what lay ahead. Even though Pete had promised her that he would not let anything happen to her, she knew that she would not be able to live if it meant being on the run from the law.

Billy and Sister bid them good night and headed for their wagon. Pete took her hand and they walked to their lean-to and sat upon the bedrolls.

"I had fun tonight," he said, wiping his brow with his kerchief. "I had a heck of a lot of fun."

"So did I, Pete. It was as if. . . ."

"What?"

"It was as if it was never going to end, and now it has."

"I think I know what you mean, Katie. It sort of has a bad feel to it to know that we'll be parting company with Billy and Sister, they've been like angels to us."

"It's more than just that, Pete. It feels like the end is coming near."

"What do you mean?"

"I don't know how to explain it exactly," she said, feeling the press of his hand in hers.

"You're worried about what happens when Billy drops us off in Mormon Springs tomorrow, aren't you?"

"Maybe so. But, I am worried about beyond that as well."

"Don't. I have already told you that we'll just ride away, make a life for ourselves somewhere. No one will ever have to know. People disappear in this country all the time."

"Pete, I have this feeling, this sense of dread about the future. I don't know how to describe it to you, but I feel that if I could have anything in the world, it would be to not let go of tonight, to not have tomorrow come."

She felt the shiver of something other than the night air pass through her.

"Pete?"

"Yes, Katie."

"I want to ask you for something."

"Sure. Anything."

"I want you to make love with me tonight. . . ."

"Katie —"

"Just say you will, Pete. Tell me you will let this night be ours to keep, no matter what happens tomorrow or the day after that."

He bent his head to her, kissed her gently. She returned his kiss. His hand stroked her hair. He whispered her name and she touched his cheek. He smelled the soft fragrance of her hair, her fingers traced lightly along his neck. He kissed her again.

"Let's not think of anything but tonight," he said.

"Yes, just tonight. Just you and me, Pete. Nothing beyond tonight."

"I love you, Katie," he whispered. "I think I loved you from the first time I saw you."

He felt the softness of her, felt the smoothness of her bare skin beneath the blanket that covered them, felt the warmth of her breathing against his neck.

"I love you too, Pete. I will love you forever, no matter what happens."

Johnny Montana sat a long time watching the camp's fire across the river. He watched as it grew dimmer and dimmer and then fade to little more than an orange glow.

The music and laughter had long since died, but not his anger. He could only imagine what the night had wrought and what was now going on between Katie and the ranger. His anger burned hot within him. He had tried to ease it with a bottle of tequila he had purchased back in Mormon Springs.

"Tomorrow," he said, swallowing some of the fiery liquor.

Unknown to either the outlaw or the those on the other side of the river, several hundred yards upstream from where Johnny Montana now sat squatting on his heels, another man waited in quiet observation of the reverie from the lighted camp.

Eli Stagg had made his way to a point enough from the camp across the river so as not to be detected, and yet close enough to study the situation.

Who those people were or what they were all about, did not matter all that much to him. He was tired and hungry and saddle sore from another day-long ride into dark. Whoever they were, they had to have grub and maybe whiskey, guns and animals. All of which would be easy larder for a man willing to take it.

The other thing they had across the river was women. It had been a fair long time since he had had a woman. The Yallar Rose had been the last, but anymore, she didn't count. Not in his book, she didn't.

Come morning, he told himself, he'd have a shot at those pilgrims, probably lay right here and pick off the ones he wanted with the Creedmore. Shoot the men, and rescue the women, he chuckled to himself. *Hell, why not!*

Chapter Twenty-five

The first light of day broke clear and clean above the encampment. The first to stir was Billy Bear Killer, with Sister McKnight stirring right along behind him.

Billy shook his head to clear all the music and some of the sipping whiskey still left over from last night's celebration. Sister seemed as bright as a new penny.

Billy climbed out of the back of the wagon, lifted his suspenders up over his shoulders, pulled on his boots, grabbed the coffee pot and walked down to the river's edge. He whistled a fiddle tune he had been playing the night before — a favorite, *Sweetwater Creek*.

He knelt by the water's edge and splashed some of the river water onto his face before dipping the coffee pot to gather coffee water.

Pete Winter was already half awake and sitting up when he heard the roar of a big bore rifle. He pushed up from the bedroll and struggled to get his trousers on.

An instant later, the wail of Sister McKnight split the air.

Katie was now fully alert and gathering her shirt about her.

"What is happening, Pete?" she cried.

"I don't know," he said, pulling his trousers on and then scrambling from the lean-to.

Running toward the wagon, he spotted Billy lying face down at the river's edge. Sister McKnight was just now reaching her fallen husband.

"Get away!" shouted the lawman as he ran toward them. Too late! A second shot roared through the dawn and splattered mud all over Sister's dress.

From downstream, where he had finally found a suitable place to cross the river, Johnny Montana heard the shots as well.

"What the hell," he muttered aloud.

For the life of him, he could not understand why anyone would be shooting in the camp. Whatever it was, he told himself, they were alerted now and he would have to make his approach with caution.

He rode the animal into the water, across a narrowing of shallows that lay in a sharp bend downstream from the camp. Cottonwoods on the other side would conceal his approach.

A third party had also heard the roar of the buffalo gun — Henry Dollar. He pulled back on the reins of the dun and listened until the first shot was followed by a second. Someone was doing some serious shooting! His instinct told him it was trouble. He put spurs to the horse and ran it full out toward the sound of the gunfire.

Pete had reached the spot next to the river where Billy lay. Sister had dropped down over him in protective fashion.

"Sister!" he shouted and pulled her away. "Katie, move her back to the wagon!" A quick check showed Billy's head and face covered with blood, but the prairie peddler was still breathing. The lawman made a fast assessment of where the shot must have come from: across the river and up on the far slope.

Whoever was doing the shooting was good at it.

Eli Stagg saw the man race toward the body of the man, saw that he had missed the woman. He watched as the two women scurried back to the wagon. Cursing his aim, he resettled the barrel of the Creedmore across the saddle.

He lowered his eye to the rear sights and brought his intended victim in line with the front bead.

Pete Winter's mind was turning quickly. Whoever it was across the river was one hell of a shot, and probably right this instant was lining *him* up for the next bullet. He dug his heels into the ground and sprinted away just as the ground where he had been kneeling exploded in a muddy spray.

Eli Stagg cursed the missed shot and quickly jacked another shell into the breech.

He saw the fellow running and before he could draw a bead on him, the target jumped in behind the wagon.

He took pressure off the trigger and settled back thinking of the missed opportunity. Except for one bad shot, he could be headed right now down to the camp, down to the women.

He turned his attention to the hobbled pair of mules whose pricked ears flicked the air.

Sister sat against a wagon wheel, her hands pulling at her hair, a high wail escaping her lips.

"Stay low, Katie. Make sure Sister stays put. Whoever that is across the river is carrying a long gun, and he can hit whatever he chooses to aim at," he warned her.

"Billy?"

"Billy's still breathing, but. . . ." He did not finish what he knew did not need to be said.

"Somehow, I have got to get to those mules and get them hitched up to the wagon. Then, we have to figure out a way to get down there and get Billy and without getting ourselves killed." He paused and caught his breath.

"I think if we can keep moving, Katie, we can keep from getting shot. Whoever is doing the shooting over there can't be all that good to hit a moving target at such a distance."

"Billy keeps his rifle in the wagon," Katie remembered.

"Katie, even if I had two good arms, that piece won't reach that fellow across the river." He saw her expectant look turn to one of disappointment.

Pete was steadying himself for a run to the mules when another shot from the big gun roared and rolled across the sky. One of the mules screamed, took a faltering step and dropped to the ground.

"Damn it! He's killing the mules!" said Pete. A second shot finished the job.

Johnny Montana had easily made it across the river. Whoever was doing the shooting was not shooting at him, he reasoned.

He worked the horse up through the stand of

cottonwoods toward the camp.

Henry Dollar had galloped up onto the rise of land overlooking the river. Across the river, at water's edge, he saw the body of a man lying face down and just beyond, a wagon. Beyond that, there was a dead mule. He had arrived just as the bounty hunter shot the second mule.

The lawman's attention was drawn to the knoll where the gun was being fired. Less than a hundred yards. He saw a blue haze of smoke rising.

He gave spurs to the dun.

Eli Stagg eyed his work on the encampment across the river. He was a patient man by nature, he could wait an hour or a day or week if need be. Sooner or later, he would have his shot at the last man and then go and take the women. With the mules shot, they weren't going anywhere.

"He holds the upper hand, Katie," cautioned the ranger. "We can't just stay here and do nothing. He knows where we are, but we don't know much about where he is. If we don't get down there to Billy, he probably won't live."

Katie fought to maintain her nerve, to stand by Pete.

"What can we do?" she asked.

"We need to maintain cover," he said. "Our only chance of getting to Billy and keeping our heads protected is if we can push this wagon down to the river ahead of us — use it for cover."

"Yes!"

"We'll have to hope the wagon rolls down in a straight line, which means you and Sister will have to push while I guide the tongue. Do you think you can do that, Katie?"

"We'll have to do it, Pete."

"Good. Let's give her a try."

They leaned themselves into the wagon, and with much effort, it began a slow movement down the slight slope toward the river.

"Push, push!" he urged.

The bounty hunter noticed the motion of the wagon. He was more curious than concerned. He considered firing a shot into the wagon itself as a warning, but prudence over the preciousness of cartridges caused him to refrain.

Several times the trio had to pause to renew their strength, each time, they adjusted the wagon's tongue and front wheels in order to guide it in the direction they wanted it to go.

Finally with one final effort, they forced their weight against the wagon and rolled it to the water's edge. Their good fortune had been to place it between the water and the body of Billy.

Pete reached Billy and just as he did so, Billy moaned and rolled over. Pete and Katie pulled him closer to the wagon. Sister began her wailing again. Quickly examining the head wound, Pete looked up with a smile of surprise.

"I think he has only been greased across his scalp and knocked cold! He's bleeding, but it looks worse than what it is."

Billy's eyes fluttered.

"Yieeee!" screamed Sister as she scrambled to him.

"It's alright, Sister. Billy's just got a new part in his hair, he'll be around in a minute."

When she saw Billy's eyes flutter all the way open, she offered him a moon-faced smile.

Eli Stagg was still concentrating on the camp below and the strange goings on when the thud of hooves snapped his attention.

Henry Dollar already had his pistol in his hand when he topped the small knoll and discovered what he had been looking for. He saw the big man lying sprawled behind the rear sights of the Creedmore.

The bounty hunter swung around, bringing the big gun to bear on the oncoming stranger. The rider looked busted up by the way he rode, but he rode coming on like the devil afire, the dun's hooves tossing up clots of dirt.

Henry Dollar saw the man swing the barrel of the Creedmore around. The rifle exploded. The slug found not the rider but the horse and buckled its forelegs. The lawman felt himself flying free of the saddle, felt the hard impact of the ground when he landed. It felt like one mighty savage blow.

The impact knocked the air from his chest, the battered ribs drove into his lungs. The pistol he had been holding flew free from his grip and was lost amid the grasses.

Instinct willed him to move. In spite of the pain and breathlessness, he struggled to his knees.

He could hear the deadly scrape of shell being jacked into the chamber of the Creedmore.

The bounty hunter was not more than ten feet from him. Standing. Lifting the big gun, the barrel glinting the morning sun. The lawman felt as though he could barely move, as though everything were in slow motion.

He heard the deep breathing of the man with the Creedmore as he approached.

From somewhere within his duster, his hand found the small pocket gun the prostitute, Janey, had bought him back in Mormon Springs.

Then, Eli Stagg made a fatal mistake. He took time to aim carefully at a man not ten feet away from him.

Henry Dollar shot the man squarely in the face. His body stiffened slightly, a few staggering steps, and his body seemed to shudder before falling forward and striking the ground.

Chapter Twenty-six

Pete Winter heard the gunfire from across the river.

Sister McKnight had washed Billy's head clean of the blood and wrapped it in a bandage of white muslin. Then she gave him a bottle of *Sorrowful Plains Elixir* to sip, which he did not seem to mind at all.

As soon as he gained back his senses and had swallowed half a bottle of elixir, he declared, "I've been pole-axed!"

"No, Billy," said Pete, "You have been shot in the head is all."

"It feels like church bells going off inside my brain!" And then, as was his manner, he offered up a slow grin that parted the upper portion of his bushy beard. "Haw, shot in the head, you say! And I lived to tell about it? Now ain't that something special!"

They all laughed and hugged one another and for a single instant forgot the danger.

"Well, this looks damn near like a party!" came the voice. Katie was the first to turn.

"Johnny!"

"That's right, darling. Ol' Johnny's come back for you. It sure as sugar looks like I wasn't missed one dern bit."

Pete Winter stood.

The outlaw leveled his gaze toward the lawman.

"I've come back, ranger. I've come back for her. No damn way in hell was I gonna let you have her. What in the hell would she do with someone like you, anyway."

He thumbed the hammer back on the pistol.

"I won't go with you, Johnny. You'll have to kill me first!"

"I can do better'n that, little Miss. I'll shoot your boy friend and them other two, then I'll do whatever in the hell I choose to do with you!"

He took aim at the ranger.

Katie stepped in front of Pete.

"Don't, Johnny! Don't do it!"

"Why the hell not?"

"Because . . . because I'm asking you not to. Let them alone and I'll leave with you."

"Don't be foolish, Katie," warned Pete.

"Shut your mouth, boy!" ordered the outlaw. "Come on ahead then, gal, climb up on the back of this animal and we'll ride out and leave them be."

She felt Pete's hand on her arm.

"Let me go," she said softly.

"Katie?"

Her eyes implored him.

"He'll kill everyone if I don't," she said. There was no doubting it. He watched as she mounted on behind the outlaw.

The mare did a little sidestep at the extra weight.

"You sure do lead a charmed life, lawman. It's the second time this woman has saved your bacon. We ever run up against each other again, I'll make sure she's not around to protect you."

Johnny Montana dug his heels into the mare and slapped it with the reins, plunging it down the slope and toward the river.

He did it without thinking.

Not until mid-stream when the water rushed up past his boots, did Johnny Montana realize his mistake, a realization brought on by an old fear — drowning.

He fought the horse's head around in order to return to shore.

Billy Bear Killer had retrieved his shotgun, and in a confused and angry state, took aim at the fleeing outlaw. Pete Winter slapped the barrels upward just as he fired both barrels.

"You'll hit Katie!"

Some of the buckshot lifted the hat off Johnny Montana's head and left him confused. He saw the old man holding the shotgun on the shoreline, cursed and fought the horse to turn back into the river.

"That dang river's full of quicksand!" warned Billy.

Henry Dollar's attention was drawn by the booming report of Billy's shotgun. He saw a man and woman on horseback struggling in the river. He saw too, the people on the far side: two men and a woman. One of the men he recognized: Pete Winter!

He did his best to organize his thoughts. Everything inside him felt busted up from being tossed from the horse.

The water had risen to their waists and then had begun to recede. Johnny Montana felt that luck was with him even though the water felt cold, like ice, like needles piercing his skin.

"Hang on, darling! This is one time when ol' Johnny beats the river!"

The mare had ridden up onto a sandbar, but then quickly sunk in to its chest, setting panic within the animal's brain.

The horse began to struggle furiously, its screams rending the air, the quicksand securing its hold all the more so with the flailing efforts.

Katie let out a soft cry of fear, and Johnny cursed, and then they were both pitched off the horse and into the river.

In an instant, Pete and Billy grabbed a rope from the wagon and plunged into the river.

"I cannot swim with one arm, Billy!"

"I larned when I was a babe," said Billy. "Give me the rope."

Henry Dollar saw that the mare was trapped and drowning in the river. He lifted the Creedmore and laid it across the bounty hunter's saddle.

He had no choice. He took aim, squeezed the trigger and ended the struggle of the horse.

Katie swam against the force pulling her downstream. She saw Billy swimming toward her, a rope looped over his shoulders.

"Hang on, sis," shouted Billy.

Johnny Montana flailed his arms, felt the river pulling him under, swallowed mouthfuls of the muddy water.

Billy could see that Katie was making headway toward the near shore and so he came and swam alongside her until they reached the shallows and could stand. Pete was already making his way down the shoreline towards them.

A terrible scream came from the river. They saw the head of the outlaw bobbing up and down, disappearing, reappearing, and then, finally, he surfaced no more.

In silent dreadful witness, Katie remembered Johnny's premonition. It had been the only thing that he had ever been right about.

Pete and Billy half-carried her back to the wagon. Sister McKnight wrapped Katie and Billy in blankets and built a fire for them to sit by. Pete stood guard with Billy's shotgun just in case the shooter across the other side decided to come on.

It was late afternoon when they heard the crack of a pistol shot. Pete glanced around the wagon. What he saw startled him.

There, sitting astride a big dun, was Henry Dollar.

Pete stepped back from behind the wagon and came to stand at the water's edge. Cupping his hand to his mouth, he shouted:

"Henry?"

The lawman nodded.

"Henry. What the hell took you so long?"

The man walked his horse into the river and crossed over.

Chapter Twenty-seven

They hitched the dun to the wagon and made their way to Mormon Springs. Five survivors who drew the stares and curiosity of the locals. Five survivors who didn't mind so much.

Sister McKnight and Billy Bear Killer bid a fond farewell to Katie, Pete, and Henry Dollar. And after their hugs and kisses and handshakes, Sister made each of them take a bottle of her *Sorrowful Plains Elixir* for their continued good health.

Sitting in a physician's office waiting for their wounds to be attended to, Henry said: "We look a sight."

"Wouldn't hardly know that we are the ones that came out ahead, looking at the two of us," said Pete.

"We need to talk, Pete."

"What about, Henry?"

"About the lady."

"If you already know, what's there to talk about."

"What're you planning on doing about her? About yourself?"

"I'm not taking her to Ft. Smith, Henry."

"Well, it's your call, son. You've thought this thing through?"

"As through as I can. The way I figure it, Henry, is that she saved my life a couple of times. That ought to be worth some consideration."

"We could both testify in her behalf if she does decide to stand trial. I reckon if we both testified, that might carry some weight. If not, we could bust her out of jail."

"You think Texas boys would stand a tinker's chance in an Arkansas court?"

"Might. You could always ask her what it is she wants."

"I have a pretty good idea already. She's a righteous woman, in spite of everything."

"Then maybe you ought to let her do what she thinks is best for herself."

"I do that, and old Judge Parker is liable to hang her. I can't see it that way."

"There comes a time in each of us when we have to do what we think is best for ourselves. You go to influencing that gal with what it is you want for her — well, it seems from the story you told me, that's the sort of thing she had with Johnny Montana."

"You think I ought to take her to Arkansas if that is what she wants?"

"I'm sure it's not what she wants," said Henry. "But, it might be what she feels she needs to do in order to live with herself."

"I reckon I need to have a talk with her then."

"I reckon it might not hurt, Pete."

"And if she decides to go to trial?"

"Then we'll all catch the stage and go back together. I'll wire the Captain and tell him the story. Maybe he could throw his hat in the ring with us if it comes to having to testify for your young lady."

"Then I'll go talk to her."

Judge Isaac Parker had a face that looked like Judgement Day: a broad flat forehead, eyes like bullets, a mouth as grim as perdition.

"Young lady," he announced in a stentorious voice. "Upon hearing the testimony of these Texas Rangers and that given by your own hand, and in light of the facts as they are now known, and furthermore, in consideration of your role in saving the life of one of these officers, I find that putting you behind bars would serve this court and its jurisdiction no good purpose. I hereby find you innocent of the charges filed against you in the slaying of State's Senator Willard Gray."

The jurist paused to mop his brow with a large blue silk kerchief.

"This weather is an abomination," he declared. "Miss Swensen, you are free to go. But, I must caution you, that not everyone in this territory may agree with my decision. Therefore it is my advice that you take your leave of this territory as soon as is convenient for you to do so." He tapped the gavel twice and dismissed his presence from the courtroom.

Pete and Katie and Henry walked outside

"Well," said Henry. "I'd just as soon get back across the river and into Texas. What are your plans?"

"We've not discussed it fully," said Pete. "But,

292

I believe we'll be getting married. After that, I always favored the country up around Smiley, over in Gonzales County. It'd be a good place to run a few head of cows. Something Katie and me could handle together."

"First, I want us to go and visit my papa back in Alabama," said Katie. "I have things I need to tell him, things I need to apologize for."

"I hope you're planning on inviting me and the Captain to the wedding," said Henry. "The Captain'll have your skin if you went ahead and took a bride without his being there."

"You'll let him know, Henry?"

"Yeah, when I get back myself."

"Trouble?"

"No, I've just got some unfinished business to take care of back up around Tascosa. I need to see a lady there. I reckon that's where I am bound soon's I can pick up a good saddle horse."

"You could catch a stage or one of the trains."

"Could, but I'd rather sit a horse. I'll have a chance to stop where I want, rest where I want, and have all the privacy I want. It'll take me longer, but I reckon I can use the time to think out what I need to."

They shook hands. Henry said, "I'd like to drop by on occasion after you get that spread of yours going — you know, just to look in on you ever now and then."

"I'd consider it an insult if you didn't, Henry."

"And so would I," said Katie.

"Well then, this is so long for now. I'll see you

293

back in Texas sometime soon."

Two hours later, as they waited for the stage to arrive, Pete Winter and Katie Swensen saw Henry Dollar riding out of Ft. Smith on a big buckskin. In spite of his injuries, he rode tall and straight, without a slump. Another thing they noticed was the fancy saddle and rig he had bought for the horse.

The saddle may have been fancy but the rider was not.

The employees of G.K. HALL hope you have enjoyed this Large Print book. All our Large Print titles are designed for easy reading, and all our books are made to last. Other G.K. Hall Large Print books are available at your library, through selected bookstores, or directly from us. For more information about current and up-coming titles, please call or mail your name and address to:

G.K. HALL
PO Box 159
Thorndike, Maine 04986
800/223-6121
207/948-2962